LIVING DOLL

by
Jane Bradley

THE PERMANENT PRESS
Sag Harbor, New York 11963

Library of Congress Cataloging-in-Publication Data

Bradley, Jane, 1955–
    Living doll / by Jane Bradley.
        p.   cm.
    ISBN 1-877946-54-0 : $22.00
    I. Title.
    PS3552.R2274L58   1995
    813'.54—dc20   94-11244
                                    CIP

First edition, September, 1995 - 1,000 copies

Manufactured in the United States of America

THE PERMANENT PRESS
Noyac Road
Sag Harbor, NY 11963

The author would like to thank the National Endowment for the Arts and the University of Toledo for support while writing this novel.

Much thanks also to Steve Boles who pushed me to tell this story, and love to Akram who made the telling easier to bear.

J. B.

"If I hadn't killed her, she would have died."
Sethe, *Beloved*
by Toni Morrison

I

When my grandfather died he had a pair of my mother's panties in his pocket: white cotton, soft-worn from my mother's three-year-old girlish round butt. There in the pocket, he could reach, rub the smooth fabric between his thumb and finger when feeling thoughtful, worried, afraid. It was a sudden death.

I never knew my grandfather. But I have felt his hand reach through time. I've felt a man's fingers part my own panties from the upper crease of my thigh, and I've looked away, pretending nothing was there, just as my mother grew up to tell us the story of how her daddy loved her so much that he died with a pair of her panties in his pocket. She was proud. She never seemed to think as I did, that there was something wrong, something missing in this story of her dead daddy's love. There was a blank page in the story, a vast blank plain that even as a girl I knew I shouldn't walk out into. Wait. How? Why? My mouth shut, eyes wide open wondering. Panties in a dead man's pocket? If my daddy died with my panties in his pocket I'd never tell the story. I would be too embarrassed. Ashamed.

When my mother was a girl she liked to bury her dolls and dig them up to bathe them in a pan of soapy water, wash their clothes, and dry them in the sun on the grass. She rocked her babies, pretended to feed them honey-suckle and sang to their wide-open blue eyes. Then compelled, she would bury them, using a spoon stolen from the kitchen to scoop the earth up and her palms to slide the dirt over their faces until they were buried from the light.

She wasn't a bad girl, not mean like her grandmother said when she'd whip her with a switch, shouting with each stroke: "One day you'll learn to appreciate things." My mother would run and sit under the pecan tree in the back yard. She would watch the sun move through the delicate lacy pattern of swaying leaves and try not to miss her daddy who was dead and her mother who never seemed to be home. She would sit, sweat mingling with tears on her face until a breeze came and cooled her as she hoped she could keep the promise and not bury her dolls again.

I never buried my babies. They were too dear and hard to come by. I needed those plastic dimpled arms, round bellies and soft heads to cuddle under covers through the nights. There was enough death in the living world to keep my dolls alive. My puppies choked on chicken bones; some were hit by cars. I cried, screaming always, teased sometimes for the ugly way my face twisted with pain. I tried to cry in private, but death is such a public thing with puppies writhing in the grass while flies and fleas buzz in summer heat. After death I calmly claimed my pets while my sisters, repulsed and angry, always ran away. I wrapped my pets in pillowcases stolen from the closet and carried them to rest in their corner in my woods.

In addition to puppies, I loved and lost my goldfish who in time always bloated and turned belly up, their tiny fish souls swimming off as I went back to Woolworth's and plunked my quarters down. Carrying pair after pair home, sloshing dully in their bags, I dumped them in the bowl and named them the eternal names of Flip and Flap, as if persistent naming could make resurrection true.

There were also turtles, tiny store-bought

things with hard backs, fragile yellow bellies, tiny claws and cool black bead eyes. Without complaint they climbed my dirt piles, swam mudhole creeks, and lived dull short lives in my turtle bowl with the spiraling ramp that ended at a flat plastic palm tree glued upright at the center like a rigid useless flag. Such lives weren't meant to be lived. But ever hopeful, I kept buying more turtles so lively and green at the start as they crawled across my hand. Then I watched them slowly wither like freshly dying leaves.

The dogs, my daddy buried; at least that is what he said. But as I watched him roll them in a plastic sheet and throw them in the back of the truck, I knew he'd toss them in a wood somewhere or throw them with our garbage at the local dump.

Some things went beyond my service. But puppies, turtles, goldfish, even after death were mine. My private graveyard was for smaller things, a little world of loss. A perfect place, a tiny space where I was too human and giant-sized to fit my thick grief in. So I shrunk the pain to a smaller scale, set a little stage of death, and reduced my sorrow to the plastic human forms of Barbie and Ken.

My momma's boyfriend, Wally, brought my first Barbie doll. He was a truckdriver and came on days my daddy worked. With daddy's twenty-four-hour fireman's shifts, Momma took the risk. Wally was a lean man with biceps that bulged like living things breathing in his arms. I couldn't help but stare at his muscles, his flashing eyes, his grin. Sometimes he'd let me run my fingertip along the thick veins that curled like snakes under his taut, tanned skin. Wally smelled like Old Spice and cigarettes and looked cleaner than my dad. He always tapped the front door, opened it, peeked with a sneaky smile, then came in. He gave us balls, jacks, Bo-Bo paddles, and Little Debbie snack cakes pilfered from his truck. Momma always took the brown paper sack he brought her with a laugh. She'd unwrap the fifth of whiskey, give him a kiss and us a look that meant we had to go. Without complaint we took our snack cakes, toys, and secrets out the door. We'd play outside under trees knowing what went on inside. We'd seen the dirty magazines underneath the bed, had squealed at the mottled skin and hairy crotches, saw that wild dog look frozen in some stranger's eyes. We knew what Wally came for, but we kept our momma's secret and our minds on the games we played until we saw Wally's truck leave and heard Momma call us in.

I knew that sex was a dirty steaming swamp

ahead. My older sister had told me it was awful, that being a girl only got worse each year once you let some boy get in. I clung to my Barbie's perfect grown-up body, its smooth flat crotch, its promise to stay pure. My Barbie was a virgin, even though she came unwrapped and plainly offered from rough truck-driving hands. Wally had pointed to the brown bubble-do hair, and the big blue eyes and said, "She looks like your momma. Why don't you call her Bobby Jo." He squeezed my Barbie in his hand, looked at me, and grinned. "No, she's Barbie," I said, reaching. I'd seen Momma naked and knew she was no doll. She had hair and fat and freckles. I'd seen her pee and bleed. My Barbie was a lady. She had money, cars, and boyfriends who only kissed with their mouths sealed off from tongues and spit. So I gripped her in both hands and stared at those sweet blue eyes. My Barbie, my real Barbie, the name-brand one. I couldn't help but smile. Now I would be like those blonde girls on TV with straight teeth, ponytails with ribbons, and nice clean clothes. They all had real Barbies and their mommas baked them cookies and never locked them out when Wally the truck-driving boyfriend came. I looked up at Wally and whispered, "Thank you, thank you,

Wally." He beamed down and said, "Take her out and play now." That time I went happily out to my place in the yard. I was reborn then into a purer world of name-brand toys like real girls in that clean bright world beyond. No more cheap pink imitation fashion doll, no more pretending I had a real Barbie with that dime-store fake Babette.

While Barbie was a debutante, Babette was local white trash. With her sluttish black-lined eyes, her lips too red and skin too pale, she looked cheap no matter how she dressed. Babette died that day I was reborn with Barbie. It was a quiet death in the back corner of my closet, with only my child's blind loyalty preventing her from being thrown away. So she remained my secret low-class self, the doll not good enough to play with Barbie, the girl I kept but hid.

Momma said she had really looked like Barbie once, before she met my dad. She said she was the kind of girl all Ken-doll boys had wanted to go out with, said she was neat and sweet and pretty back then when she was young. Momma cried when Daddy got drunk and swore, "Like Barbie, like hell, you were never nothing but a whore!" I wanted to believe she looked like Barbie with her blue eyes and bubble hairdo, but then I'd seen her laughing when Wally grabbed her butt. I'd seen her open mouth, her cheap red lips, her pale pink skin that never tanned. I knew she was no Barbie. Babette was in my blood.

But Barbie was what I could be if I practiced, prayed and tried. I planned one day to be her, but had to struggle first to make my doll look like the one in commercials on TV. She had a boyfriend, cars, houses, and at least a dozen outfits with tiny shoes that matched. She went to California beaches, New York nightclubs, sometimes even Paris, France. But my Barbie never went beyond my woods and the back yard of my house. She couldn't afford those fancy outfits. She made do with homemade clothes.

I swiped my family's socks to make them, cut them down to tube-shaped dresses, shirts and skirts. I snipped armholes, added buttons, rickrack, ribbons, glitter, glue. I used my pink lace-edged Easter socks for her cocktail dress and loved the girlish ruffle stretched across her rock-hard breasts. The sexy cocktail dress was my most prized creation until I saw Flash Gordon on TV one day and was inspired to higher realms in my design. I ran to my mother's kitchen, swiped a roll of foil, found scissors,

tape, and glue, then hid for hours in my bedroom, where in all flashing crinkling glory, my
Space Barbie was born.

First, I wrapped her in press-on foil pants,
made a halter top and used Scotch tape to se-
cure her flowing cape. I made a mini-skirt and
a straight shift dress that glistened above her
silver press-on boots. I added foil wrist ban-
gles, and when her hat fell off I stuck it on
with a pin rammed in her head.

Space Barbie came from Mars. She knew the
secrets of the universe and flew above the daily
trauma of dead pets, secret boyfriends and my
momma and daddy's fights. But she didn't visit
often. She had better things to do out there
with stars and angels, her visitations holy days
that couldn't come too often or they'd lose the
magic that could lift me from my world. So
most days she was plain bubble-do Barbie in
her clothes of cut-up socks. She was happy
with her shoebox house, had a good life, never
once got hit or hurt or sick. And she had Ken
to talk to when I sealed them up at night in
their cozy shoebox home. I never thought to
bury them. They weren't worth the trouble
since they never really died. They'd always be
alive above ground, promising an eternal pres-
ent without age, loss, or pain. They always

smiled, never argued with my plans and so became the perfect tools of grief for the mortal living dying ones, my pets.

My graveyard was scaled down with paths just wide enough for the dainty steps of Barbie and the flat bare feet of Ken. Mourning clothes always meant the risk of black socks stolen from Daddy's drawer. I sneaked in when Momma was out, pushed through the rolled lumps of socks to finger his heavy silver dollars, dirty playing cards, and rubbers wrapped in foil. I held in secret my fascination for the grown-up man things he only thought he hid. But I justified my theft claiming proper death had a higher purpose and thinking things couldn't really be stolen from a family with a blood connection. Lost things weren't really lost; they simply moved around. I knew he'd never miss those socks and I was safe since Momma was too busy with Wally and whiskey on the days Daddy worked to notice what I did.

I hid Barbie's grieving face with a veil cut from the toe of Daddy's sock. She walked the pebble-lined path as I held and slowly guided her to the gravesite with my right hand, and Ken followed barefoot in my left. They stood balanced in my grip above the open grave and grieved.

A girl finds comfort in her small worlds: shoebox houses, tiny toys, and painted castles in the bottom of fish bowls. A girl needs a kind of small-scale peace in a house where yells, smells and secret things are too thick to grasp. So I reached for what I could hold in my quiet careful hands. A living doll, they called me for my sweetness, silence, cuteness, my ease at being good. I knew from my baby dolls how to do it, how to smile and eat and drink and sleep and pee on cue. A "living doll" they called me, but I knew that underneath the plastic my blood breathed, heart pounded, belly moved. Just like my puppies, I could cry and choke and bleed. I could die like my dead things, and once buried I would rot. I knew I was a creature more like my puppies that rotted when they died, that I was nothing like those dolls. But I thought if I could be like Barbie, no one would tease or hurt. If I could be like Barbie, some larger hand would always hold me safe above an open grave, and I would never die.

So I played my graveyard game and kept my private line between the living and the dead, split myself between the smiling sunlight side and the rank decay of graves. I lined the little graveyard paths with bright pebbles, and transplanted mosses, violets, and wild strawberries. I watered, loved them, but they never seemed to grow. In time they always died.

I dug neat graves and wrapped my dead in clean bright cloths. Then as I offered my pets to the ground like little presents, Barbie and Ken mourned. They carried bouquets of honeysuckle rubber-banded tightly to their stiff and outstretched hands. They stood at the gravesite the proper time for grief. Then I laid them on the ground with their rigid arms reaching, and eyes staring up at treetops as I scooped the dirt back slowly into graves with my spoon. I held Ken and Barbie upright in my hands and prayed. Then I carefully peeled the wilting clumps of honeysuckle from their hands and let Barbie place the flowers on the grave. Finally I shoved a Popsicle stick cross for a headstone in the dirt. I knew the first rain would knock it down, but I loved the daily tending of my graveyard the way I'd seen my momma tend her petunias and red pepper plants. My dead pets were my garden; Barbie, Ken, and stolen socks and spoons my tools.

And so I wanted to be my Barbie who seemed happy in her sock clothes. When my dog chewed her head flat, the face bounced back and smiled. She could stand all day at a graveside and stay pretty, sweet and upright as long as I could hold her in my sweaty, gripping hands.

Barbie taught me death was not a sequence, no cycle of darkness and light made by some sad girl's need to dig holes with stolen spoons. I knew my mother's claim was wrong that scooping dirt from her dead doll's mouth meant she was revived. For me death was a dark division made in private shadows of my head and heart, not a cycle as my momma thought but a constant shifting border like the horizon that stood rolling between the earth and sky.

A mortal girl, I went down and died a little with my puppies, turtles, goldfish. The hurt part stayed buried with the pain and love and hunger blocked with each little scoop of dirt. But the living doll girl stayed above ground, stiff and smiling. I knew mortal things were too ugly to be left above, too stinking full of blood and bugs and rot. There was a future with my Barbie, a life that felt no pain with that hollow heart and head. So I lived on, like Barbie, stayed above ground, steady, and forgiving, so sweet and pretty sometimes they would swear I was alive.

*　*　*

My mother used to sing for doughnuts. On Saturdays she rode the bus downtown, her weekly outing with her mother who worked all week at the Moon Pie factory, day in, day out carrying the scent of sugar and oil on her clothes. Her mother sat at the counter and drank cup after cup of black coffee, while my mother sat politely rocking back and forth on her stool, never spinning around because that wasn't ladylike. She contented herself with gripping the counter in both hands and pushing herself gently left and right, feeling the sway of the stool beneath her, imagining how it would feel to spin all the way around. Finally her mother would finish the coffee and tell my mother that it was time to go.

My mother never said she was bored, restless, ignored. She told me that as she walked into the doughnut shop, the man behind the counter would say, "Morning, Bobbie Jo, you gonna hop up here and sing?" Someone would lift her up. Then standing on the counter, she would clasp her hands at her waist, sway a little with the beat in her head, and sing what she could remember of "Chattanooga Choo Choo." She told the story with a quiet light in her face, a peaceful smile pulling at her lips as if these moments of standing on a counter and singing for a sweet were a piece of heaven in a life of rationed sugar, butter, and bread, and a mother who always worked at the factory, who day in, day out smelled of those sick sweet Moon Pies.

I used to love to hear my mother tell this story, would request it again and again. As she fingered, fondled, loved and sucked down the memory as if it were a piece of butterscotch candy, I would listen, watching, clinging to every word, charmed, but knowing that I would never do that. I would never stand on a counter where everyone could see my panties. I would never sing for a doughnut. I would be too embarrassed. Ashamed.

* * *

My mother named me Shirley, for Shirley Temple, she said. I taught myself to tap dance, made myself look bright-eyed, practiced in the mirror how to be a darling thing. It worked. "Sweetest little thing that ever drew breath," my mother told me as she dressed me and curled my hair. She bought me matching lace socks and lacy-bottomed panties, shined my patent-leather shoes with Vaseline and took me out, the model child, the only one of her children she took to lunch to show off to the grown-ups, her badge of the good mother she claimed she was. They would smile at my big brown eyes, face like a doll, and offer me things just for being sweet: a nickel, a peppermint, a piece of Juicy Fruit gum.

They all said it, friends and strangers would shake their heads and say: "She looks just like Shirley Temple, ain't she the sweetest little thing." I was trained to be, had to be a darling ray of sunshine, a perfect angel of a girl. I knew the danger of a rule broken, a cry of selfishness or rage: a scream, or smack, or worse. So like Shirley Temple, I learned to step forward, my mouth fixed in a cute pout when angry, a comic frown that I could transform to a smile on demand. I was Shirley, a living doll, they said, just like Shirley Temple. How my sisters must have hated me.

My mother bragged that when I cried as an infant, her raised hand alone could make me stop. I must have been a smart baby to know the sign and consequence of that raised hand. I was rarely whipped—the belt curled in my mother's purse was enough warning for me. I could feel it lashing at the back of my legs while my mother held my arm, me trying to run as she gripped me and we turned round and round in a circle, my mother at the center turning with me as I tried to run away.

I can still remember the time she slapped my face so hard I fell off the kitchen stool. I had talked back, had told her I was going to play at Kathy's house when she had just told me no. "Don't you ever talk like that to me!" One flicker of will, and a slap that took my breath, sent me to the floor, a time I took the hit, didn't have a chance to see the hand raised.

*   *   *

I never knew my daddy, but carried the legal name of my older sister's daddy, Jack Stone. "Daddy Jack" I called him, but my sister, Ruby, had the high cheek bones, that rich coffee skin of her daddy's Native American blood. I was fair, with a face like the Little Dutch girl on the can of powdered cleanser. I didn't look like Ruby in the least, nothing like the daddy they said was mine.

I didn't belong to my step-daddy either. The father of my little sister Sally and my brother Glenn, he dated my mother when I was a baby. He took me on dates with them, treated me like his own at the start, fed me cups of vanilla ice cream, then later peanuts and popcorn. This was the man I felt was my daddy, the one who taught me numbers, who kept treats for me in the glove compartment of his truck, the one who showed me card tricks, taught me to catch a fish with a cane pole, let me play all I wanted with the carton of worms.

I had the legal name of one daddy, loved the man who raised me, but never knew my own. Like a doll rolling off the assembly line, no single pair of hands made me. I was adjusted, attended to, made, and sent on. My legal daddy belonged to my sister. He took her places, brought her presents, brought me something once: a big stuffed Yogi Bear when he brought Ruby the Huckleberry Hound. A sudden gesture of equal affection, but it was Ruby he spent the day with. I stood at the window and watched them back out the driveway, Ruby bouncing behind the windows of his shiny blue car. Later I would stare at the huge stuffed Yogi Bear, watch the wide open friendly plastic brown eyes. I knew a piece was missing. My mother was my mother; I had two daddies, one by name, one by habit, but even then I knew something was wrong. I was fifteen before I learned the name of my blood daddy, the man who came in between.

* * *

I was in my mother's car once, watching the sky change. I was waiting. She had picked me up at the bus stop, said she wanted to run into a place just for a minute. "You've got a snack," she said. She tossed me the keys and said, "Listen to the radio a little if you want to, but not too long or you'll run the battery down." I watched the sky fade from bright blue to gray to purple night when the neon lights flashed on. I saw the letters *V. F. W.* in red block letters above the blackened glass door. I knew it was a bad place, knew it was where the man I called my daddy went to drink. They went dancing there sometimes and always came back in a fight.

I watched a small square window behind black bars. I saw a Miller beer sign in gold letters and the blinking red, white and blue colors of a neon can of Pabst Blue Ribbon.

I ate the peanut butter cheese crackers she'd bought me and drank the bottle of Coke. My snack became my supper. In the dark I wondered what my sisters ate for dinner, wondered if she called them and told them we'd be late coming home.

She was still in there. I'd been watching. I

saw her tight blue dress go in the black glass door under the V. F. W. sign. I sat, stared at the letters, squinted my eyes together to see the color bleed like red ink spilled across a table. I squinted until the letters melted to a pool of color, then compressed into one thin line. I kept at it as long as I could, until I couldn't deny my hunger and my need to pee. I tried not to think about it, and I kept my eyes closed.

I felt the cold hard push there up under my belly and kept telling myself it wouldn't be much longer, that she had to come out soon. Unless she'd forgotten. But she'd remember, it was a school day. She had picked me up at the bus stop and left me in the car with only crackers and a Coke. Surely she couldn't forget.

I turned on the radio, told myself she would be back before the end of five songs, but I'd played this game already, once right after she went in, then two times more. I watched the door for movement. Two men went in, a woman with teased red hair. Five songs. She'd come, she had to; I had to pee and bit my lip to keep from crying, told myself if it got real bad I'd pee outside. But it was dark and I couldn't see where I'd do it. I was afraid to go behind the building, and I couldn't do it in the parking lot. Not even a dog would want to pee in a parking lot. Even dogs need a tree, a wall, a clump of grass.

I turned off the radio, squeezed the car keys in my hand. I wondered if I'd explode if I held it long enough. Ruby had told me it happened sometimes. "Just like a water balloon," she had said. "If you hold it too long, you'll explode."

I opened the car door, stepped out, and crouched down, the partly open door pressing against my shoulder. I tried to imagine myself pulling down my panties, my butt bared in the night, my pee gushing splashing against my legs and spreading out into a puddle around my shoes. I couldn't do it. I slipped back in the car, closed the door and cried in little sobs, not tears, just sob sounds tearing at my throat. I looked in the back seat for a cup, a bottle, anything I might pee in. But there was only my Coke bottle, and I'd never get it right. I'd miss, and the pee would splash all over my hands, make a mess all over the car. My mother would smell it, and she'd whip me, tell everybody about the time Shirley peed in the car like a dog. I couldn't do that. I'd be too ashamed.

I wondered if somehow my mother had left when I wasn't looking. Was she sick inside? Had she fallen down dancing? Did someone hit her head and leave her knocked out in a corner on the floor?

I could see it in the paper: "Girl explodes in car. Mother found dead." Everyone would know. Ruby would laugh: "I told you, I told you, I told you. If you hold it long enough, you'll explode."

I got out of the car and walked up to the black glass door. I stood there, counting to twenty, giving her one last chance to come out. I could smell the smoke and beer, hear the twanging of the jukebox, the talking laughing dancing noise. Using both hands, I pushed the door open, stepped inside, and was swallowed by the thick warm air, the darkness and smoke, the white faces that floated like nightmares above my head. The faces turned, froze, stared down at me. A path opened as I walked slowly, looking up, trying to find my mother's face in the crowd. They were silent and stepped back from me as if I were some spirit that suddenly appeared. I kept moving, watched the walls for a bathroom door. Surely the women had to pee sometime. I wondered why my mother didn't remember how Coke always made me need to pee.

Then I saw her. She was sitting on a man's lap at a table, her dress pulled up, her thighs

26

huge and white, the skin bulging a little over the tight band of her stockings. She frowned, stared at me, then jumped up, grabbed me by the arm and pulled me toward the wall. Her fingers stung my arm. She whispered low and mean, "I told you to wait! I told you I'd be right back, damn you!"

I couldn't stop crying. I tried to say it, but they were listening. She shook my shoulders and stared at my face. I saw the wrinkles, straight lines between her eyebrows, thin and hard. She said, "What the hell is the matter with you?"

I took a breath, tried to say it clearly so she'd understand and stop yelling. "I. Have. To. Go. To—" She yanked me hard then pushed me through a door.

Inside there was a black-haired woman smoking a cigarette. Another one was putting on lipstick. They both stared at me. I turned away, keeping my head down as I moved toward the wooden door of the stall. I locked the door and sat on the toilet. Leaning forward, I tried to pee, but it wouldn't come out.

"What's that kid doing in here?" one of the women said. Then I heard laughter, and finally the creak of the closing door. I closed my eyes, straining until I could feel the hot release.

A doll can be put away in a closet. A doll doesn't need to be fed. It doesn't cry when the sometimes loyal turn away; it stands there, face blank, a benevolent smile maybe, palms patiently waiting for the next offering whenever, however it may come. A doll has no voice, makes no demands. A doll is a dead thing. It never needs to pee.

Appetite was Shirley Temple's only bodily function. Or a thin gloss of sweat maybe to be wiped with her chubby forearm as she paused in a dance routine. Sweat maybe, hunger, a need for sleep, but not once did I see her need to pee. I sat on the couch with chocolate milk and peanut butter crackers and watched Shirley win hearts and break obstacles with her pouting lips, sweet voice and round cheeks. *Our Little Girl* taught me the reward of a girl's struggle to keep her parents from divorce. She won, of course, with her luck, faith, and smile. She declared in the end, "Oh it's the best, the best ever." She posed her reunited parents for a picture, wouldn't allow her mother to cry from relief. Shirley shook her finger and said, "You're not supposed to cry, Mommy. You're supposed to smile and laugh." Mommy smiled on cue, and the picture sealed the promise that in Shirley's world all was well.

I watched her movies and followed the camera to her panties, clean white cotton panties, her little round butt. Her face always beamed when men lifted her, twirled her, held her, cuddled, kissed, the camera always holding that butt and her soft sweet lips. "Why do we keep seeing her panties?" I asked my mother once. She smiled and kissed my head and said simply, "Because a little girl's panties are cute."

Not to me. I wouldn't show my panties to no camera, no man, nobody. I kept seeing my mother's white cotton panties hidden in her daddy's pocket where in secret, in public, his thumb and finger could reach in the dark folds to fondle and rub.

At his funeral someone lifted my mother from behind and told her to kiss her daddy goodbye. She did it. She leaned from the waist and stretched to kiss those lips that burned her skin with chemicals that had been pumped in to hold off decay. She kissed, jumped back from the cold stiff feel of him, then ran crying. She said her lips burned and peeled for days.

* * *

29

I hear my uncle saying, "Don't that feel good, don't that feel good?" I can't speak. I nod as he smiles at me, moistens his fingers in his own mouth, pushes again under the elastic of my panties and wiggles, breathing on me as he probes his way in.

"Daddy Gene," my legal daddy's brother, liked to do it at the kitchen table. He'd sneak under it, slide his finger up my shorts into my panties and wag the finger back and forth slowly in between. He was sneaky when my sisters were around, more bold when he was supposed to be taking care of me. "Y'all go on; I'll watch Shirley," he'd say when they went off to the farmers' market and left me with him alone. He was a policeman. He wore a black leather holster and smelled like the oil of gray metal handcuffs, the slick heavy gun. He let me load it once, let me palm those heavy bullets, roll them, feel the slick solid weight of lead, slide the copper-based, silver-tipped shape of them into the chambers as I sat on his lap at the kitchen table. I felt him breathing, then slid off his legs to get away from the smell of his sweat.

On one arm he had a tattoo of a girl in a bathing suit, her breasts spilling out across the

brown muscle of his arm and on the other arm
a heart with my aunt's name curled at the center: "Sweet Sue." He had an ashtray he kept
by his chair in the living room, a naked woman
lying on her back, her ceramic white limbs
sprawled long and open. You put the cigarette
out in her crotch and smoke would curl up
through tiny holes in her breasts. He would
demonstrate laughing: "Ain't that something,
now ain't that something else?"

He held me, his shoulders bare, muscles and
chest damp with sweat under that white tank
undershirt cut to show his hair curling, his
muscled tattooed arms. "Don't that feel good,"
he'd whisper needing only one hand to hold
me, keep me still where he spread me on the
table, scooped at me sliding back and forth
with his finger, then his tongue, whiskered
face rough against my thigh as he lapped at
me. "Don't that feel good?"

His arm jerked at his open pants, the belt
buckle jangling, slapping a metal sound
against the rim of the red Formica table. I
turned my head, stared at the calendar on the
wall, saw the smiling face of the girl in the
yellow bathing suit bent over a little, butt
round and high from the push of her high-
heeled sandals, breasts pushing the limit of the

yellow cloth barely held together by a yellow bow. She was smiling for the camera, tiny white teeth, pearly, like the teeth of my baby doll. The table rocked hard against the back of my head, so hard I couldn't feel him, only smell the sweat of him, the table pressing as my head rocked back and forth with the push of his head. I thought of puppies pushing at the teats of our dog with their paws as they sucked, eyes closed, mouths pink and milky. I thought of puppies as his head moved against me, and I stared at the girl in the bathing suit, red mouth smiling. "Don't that feel good?" I tried not to feel the table, hard and rocking, metal squealing as it hit the wall and pushed, pushed, pushed into the back of my head.

I tried to be the girl who beamed "just like Shirley Temple," the living doll. I tried to force the face of Shirley Temple over my face, the Shirley who sometimes ran screaming in circles, shaking her hands as if burned, the girl who threw up almost daily, the girl who once on the way to Daddy Gene's house yanked the chrome handle of the car door and tried to throw herself out. No matter how tough the story got, Shirley Temple would never do such a thing as that. It was my sister, Ruby, who grabbed me, pulled me in as my Daddy stamped on the brakes. "The door flew open," I said, big-eyed, staring up at them, while seeing in my head the black asphalt flying under, reaching up, moving like a fast dark river. Suddenly I knew it would have hurt. The road would have cracked my skull wide open, would have burned and torn away my skin.

II

My mother believed in spirits. She taught us that it was a common thing to be possessed by something, a demon, a force, a wandering soul looking for some moist soil, an open wound in someone where it could take root and grow. My mother told me sometimes she thought my daddy was possessed. How else could a man have the strength to rip a dishwasher from the wall, the door twisted, metal hinges bent? He tore it, lifted it, somehow threw it into the back yard. We later played with it, put our Barbie dolls in it, gave them rides on the round plastic-coated glass rack, sending them flying, limbs stiff as they stared ahead into the air, spinning around.

Possession. That explained things, why sometimes my daddy who flipped pancakes high in the air just to make me laugh, could suddenly in a rage throw a cat flat against the wall or circle the house, yelling, shooting his hunting rifle at the house. Possession. That explained why he'd pull me on his lap and cover my mouth, choke me with a deep wet kiss that took my breath away with the smell of beer, sweat, his cigar, his stubbled face tearing at my cheek. I would walk away wiping the wetness from my mouth with the back of my hand, and put a cool rag to my burning face. I'd walk, silently, down the hall, out the door, in whatever direction seemed safe.

Possession. That explained why Daddy Gene would sometimes hold me, the hard table rubbing a knot into the back of my head, why he made me nod yes, mouth tight, jaw clenched to his demand, "Don't that feel good?"

Possession explained why my mother who taught me about guardian angels could suddenly turn mean. She shined my shoes, curled my hair, starched my dresses so they'd stand out like Shirley Temple's. She bought me lace panties to match the lace on my soft thin smooth nylon socks. She rocked me, stroked her fingers lightly on my back until I fell asleep. Only possession explained why some nights suddenly she'd pull the covers off of us, yelling, "Get up and find my bottle! Get your asses out of that bed!" I thought it was demons who came and hid the whiskey for a trick.

35

They took over my mother and made her face twist like that, made her scream, and stand in the kitchen and stare. We looked under cushions, felt the backs of drawers, reached under the sink, or behind the canned soup in the cabinets. We looked everywhere until one of us called, "I found it." She'd walk hard across the floor, footsteps shaking the walls, grab the bottle, and without a word walk away. We would stand there looking at each other, relieved. Then hearing her quietly make a drink in the kitchen we would crawl back into our bunk beds, turn off the lights, and clutch a few more hours sleep. Possession. Only demons could make the ones who loved me do such things.

Sunday mornings my mother watched *The Oral Roberts Show.* I sat next to her, bare feet curled under me as I nestled at her side. With her arm around me, we stared at the black and white TV screen and watched the Reverend Oral Roberts grip the victims' heads between his hands and tearfully pray, squeeze and sway the rocking victim with his tight hands. Sometimes I thought he would twist their heads off, and the demon would suddenly leap out in a cloud of smoke. I waited to see the devils let loose on TV, but it never happened. The victims were young, old, men, and women. Some throwing off crutches, rising and running out of wheelchairs, would be healed. The possessed babbled, screamed, shook, and foamed at the mouth, spitting strings of spit. They were spitting demons out, my mother told me, but it only looked like strings of spit to me. The TV doesn't show it right, she said, and I believed her. I believed when suddenly the victims stopped fighting and tearfully hugged Oral Roberts, thanking Jesus for setting them free.

My mother also believed that some people were blessed. Sometimes she said I was a cursed child, and other times she said I was the greatest blessing she ever had. She held me in her arms, saying I was a gift from God and that at any instant he could snatch me away. She said I was a "sickly" child and had to be careful, that I was open to infections, damaged, fragile, weak. My bad health was her warning, like the screaming voice of my grandmother: "One day you'll learn to appreciate things!" My mother would hold my head between her hands and pray with Oral Roberts. Once she made me put my hand on the TV screen against the image of Oral Roberts' healing hand held up to the camera. I knelt before the TV to let his blessing cross through the humming black and white dots on the cold glass surface of the screen.

Momma said I was her ray of God's light in a storm. That was why she named me for Shirley Temple, the girl who could make anyone smile. I thought then all children were blessings that came by being wished for, by eating magic fruit, striking a deal with a dwarf, or throwing a caught fish back to the sea. Babies came by magic and were lost only when evil ones stole them for some selfish purpose. I was my mother's blessing, almost lost, but spared. I was a blessing who had to wrestle my way into this world, claim a womb, then emerge to spend my life struggling to prove my worth.

The year of my conception my mother's sister died of a stroke, her brother shot his head off, and her own mother was dying from tumors growing like wild pears through her womb. My mother had one baby named Ruby, an ex-husband who had beaten her and left. She had boyfriends, some married, some not, always on their way to someone, someplace else. She had two back alley abortions, from an old woman with red hair who claimed to have been a nurse at some time, a nurse who wore an apron embroidered with a rooster crowing, the black words "Cock-a-doodle-do!" curling above the red rooster's head thrown back. The woman moved around the kitchen table, hooked my mother's bare feet into the rungs of straight-backed chairs. My mother had closed her eyes and breathed the smell of fatback and beans cooking on the nurse's stove, while the woman jabbed at the swollen cervix, tore enough to start the bleeding, then sent my mother home.

But this was not to happen a third time. The legend was: My dying grandmother takes my mother's arm just as she prepares to leave for the "nurse," with me sprouting inside. She is on her way again to see the rooster. My grandmother stops her and swears: "If you have this child, she'll be your greatest blessing!" So the story goes. More likely my mother just couldn't bring herself to curl her feet around the rungs of those chairs, spread her legs, and lie back again on that kitchen table. So I came into the world, wrestled my way out, nearly died born breech, trapped and strangling for a time in the birth canal. Finally, I came through wailing and screaming to the world that slapped me with the cold dry air the way sunlight must slap and stun the moist, slick gills of a fish on someone's hook.

My mother's skin smelled like fresh bread. I can see her scattered freckles, her bluish veins untangling from her wrist reaching up the soft whiteness of her inner arm. I curled into her, tried to slow my breathing, match my breath with her long sleep sigh. I watched the lights move in her opal ring, trapped spirits, I thought, playing, dancing somehow, caught in a ring, trapped and playing under the shimmering cold stone dome.

*   *   *

They say when I was a toddler, they tied bells on my high-topped white shoes so they could listen for where I was in the house, so they could find me and keep me from tearing off the heads of Ruby's paper dolls. It was my only mean habit as a child. I was the good one, I heard Momma say, trying to convince my sister that my destruction was more out of curiosity than rage. But Ruby, round-faced, sneered: "Shirley's not good; she's just sneaky." She knew a good girl didn't need bells on her shoes as a warning to paper dolls. A good girl didn't slap her little sister, Sally, a blue-eyed, curly-headed baby that I slapped once when she wouldn't give me back my doll. Shirley Temple never slapped anyone. Her anger was righteous indignation at worst. She was a "Little Princess" who even when orphaned, abandoned, and insulted still found room in her heart to give and be happy for anyone else's love. Even when all facts told "Shirley" that her daddy was killed at war, she insisted, "Oh no, my daddy isn't dead." Denial worked for her; the plot always proved her right. Daddy was found, all was well, and she beamed with living confirmation of her faith as the movie faded out.

Denial. It worked for Shirley, but I wondered if she ever screamed, slapped, tore and broke something when the camera wasn't on her face. What happened to Shirley when her short skirt flounced off the screen and she disappeared from our view into another room? I ripped off the heads of paper dolls in the back room, though I sang like a teapot and tap danced in the kitchen. I was the good girl who could read, write, add, subtract, and spell, but I tore off those paper doll heads given the chance, and muffled the sound of the bells ringing with my knotted sock so no one could hear me sneak down the hall. Ruby knew.

41

Ruby, my sister with her smirk, three years older, who already knew the fingers, cock, and tongue of the policeman, our uncle, Daddy Gene.

I see her somber, round eight-year-old face. She was bigger, older, smarter, played football with the boys, read books, could count to ten in Spanish. She could make hot chocolate and Jell-O by herself. I would watch with envy as she walked down our gravel driveway to catch the bus to school. I listened for the bus to come rumbling up the road, heard the squeal of brakes, watched the clanking miracle of the folding glass door that opened and waited as she stepped up inside. Then the door closed as the bus rolled forward, carrying her away.

Afternoons I would sit at the end of the driveway waiting for the bus to bring her home. If she was late, I'd worry. She'd told me about the narrow dirt road the bus took over mountains, the turn-around point where the bus had to stop, back up, and turn on the edge of a cliff. I'd jump up at the first flash of school-bus yellow up the road between the trees. I'd stand, eager to carry her books up the hill of the driveway, and daily I'd ask her what happened, what were the others kids like, what

did she learn at school. She'd tell me something to silence me, some little fact like they
grow oranges in California, bananas in Brazil.
I'd carry her books in, and while we sat at the
table having chocolate milk and cookies, I'd
page through her books, run my fingers over
the colored maps of countries, follow diagrams
of the water cycle, study the carefully arranged
photographs of the four food groups. "I can't
wait to grow up," I'd say as I watched her walk
away from the table and go turn on the TV.
Once she simply stood, pushed the papers
across the table, shook her head, looked down
at me, and sighed, "You don't want to grow
up. It just gets worse and worse every year."

I ran from the room crying. She wasn't jok-
ing. She'd teased me before, but this time she
meant it. It wasn't a trick. She knew we were
all getting older, and it would be awful. I ran to
my mother who was outside hanging clothes,
grabbed her thighs, and stood crying until she
bent and held me to her chest.

Those were the good days. That is how a
child remembers things, good days, bad days,
good mom, bad dad, good girl, good girl, good
girl. That is how a child knows things. That is
me. The good days: A gravel road down a hill,

over the cornfield, across the railroad track, and alongside Chickamauga Creek where my best friend Kathy Hanes had to fetch water from the spring.

The good days: A nice brick house, the only one on that new gravel road, cows in a pasture next door. Kathy Hanes and her house with no running water, just a walk and a slide down the red rocky hill, Kathy Hanes whose momma wrung the chicken's neck and plucked it for her chicken and dumplings. The white flesh and doughy dumplings bubbled up in her pot, the picked bones set aside in a bowl for me and Kathy to salt and suck while we waited to eat. We sat on the back porch, legs dangling off rough boards as we swung our feet, looked out at the creek, and threw bites of cold biscuit down to the chickens who clucked and squawked, pecking at the ground. They walked filling up and fattening as Kathy and I made bets on which one would be the next to be plucked and put in her momma's pot.

Georgia Hanes had white-gray hair, blue eyes, red, man-looking hands. Kathy bragged that the song "Georgia" was written for her momma. A believer, I figured her momma had been pretty once, before she married, before

44

her husband beat her, before she got stretched out and wrinkled from having all those kids. I would watch her heating water, breaking the bones of a chicken, and I'd wonder how she had come to this. Kathy Hanes' momma had been the reason for a famous song, and now she was living in a house with no running water and a husband that sometimes beat her with a belt.

Mr. Hanes was tanned and skinny, and he made me think of brown spiders. He beat them all with a belt, even Georgia. I can see him, leathery face always frowning, his hands tough and strong. I feared he could snap our necks like chickens if he ever got the urge.

As he came in the house I watched for a sign of his mood, could smell it as soon as he pushed open the door, and I saw the thin lips slightly twisting, ice-gray eyes red-rimmed from drinking on the way home from work. He glanced around the room and looked for something, anything to give him a reason to yell, to unbuckle and start swinging that thick black belt.

Kathy and I ran and hid in the chicken house. We held our breath against the sour dead smell of rotten eggs. We watched the house through the cracked door, listened for the yelling until finally something eased over or gave way inside. We'd sit and tell stories, watch the chickens and wonder if they did it like people: his thing sticking in her thing. How did they do it? We'd look at their round bodies, scrawny legs, the roosters always strutting outside, the hens inside in the dark stinky shed with us, all of us staring blankly at the dust hanging in the light like dead dirt suspended in the air, floating and trapped within the limits of the shed.

Those were the good days. I was voted princess of Hillcrest Elementary School, wore a dress of white satin, white netting, just like Cinderella. More good days: three-layer birthday cakes, pink roses, the crusty dried edges of colored icing—we almost gagged from those roses so thick and sweet in our throats. Momma's petunias growing along the sidewalk, trips to Florida in the white Rambler, me, Ruby, Momma, and the man I called daddy, his own children not yet born. But everything was sliding. The birthday cake slipped; the walls swayed, the windows crashed. And I woke to see that it wasn't dreams of evil or too much thick sweetness that made me choke on what I swallowed, made me cry, turn my head away, and gag.

That year, a week before Christmas, our nice brick house burned. I had thought brick didn't burn, that it couldn't fall down, thought I was as safe as the third little pig. My friends in the wood houses had naked light bulbs, peeling wallpaper, leaking roofs and daddies that came in swinging a belt. But not me. I was a princess in a nice brick house. My daddy flipped pancakes, and my momma made my dresses and curled my hair.

Ruby and I were at our grandmother's who lived in Georgia next door to Daddy Gene, Daddy Gene who daily parted my legs at the kitchen table, where I was trying to shape bears and turtles out of blue and green Play-Doh. "That feels good don't it. Don't that feel good?" So I stayed close to Ruby. We stuck close, played and ate together, slept together as much as we could.

We were on the living room floor, drawing clothes for paper dolls, dolls with their heads on when our grandmother came in the room and told us the news. We looked up and knew something was awful by the way she stood shaking her head, wringing that blue-checked dish cloth in her hand. "Your house burned, honey," she said, and I looked at Ruby as if it must be her house somehow without being mine. Ruby got up and ran across the room, but I sat there coloring a green party dress for my black-haired paper doll. "The dress won't fit," Ruby had told me. I'd drawn the dress too big, as if somehow by will, when finished, I could shrink the colored paper down to size.

Someone was crying somewhere. Ruby was crying on the phone. I ran out, headed for the swing under the live oak in the back yard. But I saw my grandmother running toward me, and Daddy Gene coming with her, tucking his shirt in his pants as he walked toward me, and I wondered what he was doing at home in the daylight. Why was he tucking in his shirt like that, the belt buckle hanging loose as he picked me up and said, "Let Daddy Gene hold you, you poor little thing"?

I tried to see how the house burned from the scattered details I heard: Mother rocking my brother Glenn to sleep, watching the opening scene of *F. B. I.*, my sister Sally eating Cheerios off the coffee table, still awake and up late that night. Daddy was in the bathroom. Suddenly, he said, he smelled burning plastic and wires, saw the smoke peel from the ceiling, and he ran to get the family out. They stood in the cold night watching the house burn, our Christmas presents securely hidden at my grandmother's house, and our family treasures safely packed in the trunk of the car.

I went back there after Christmas, a gray January day, wearing my red galoshes and blue corduroy pants, hands bare and pink with cold. But I didn't feel my hands, only what my hands felt with the stick as I poked through the ashes, beams, and soggy remains of plastic, cushions, glass, and metal pans. With big high steps for my small legs, I stepped over charred brick, the remains of walls crumbling. A blackened shell of sharp cold air and gray ash. It was a thorough burning. Took everything we could claim on insurance forms. We were lucky to have survived. "Ain't that peculiar," a neighbor said. "A fireman's house burning down." He stood with us and watched the man I called my daddy who wouldn't take his eyes off the black beams, boards and ashes on the ground. "An electricity fire too," he said. He shook his head. I saw the look. "Imagine that! A fireman and electrician's house burning down!"

I saw the three-layered birthday cake burning, the yellow flames on the candles, the long curls of black smoke. I saw my long curls momma placed around my head like Shirley

Temple, the starched dresses, crinolines, lace socks and panties, the shiny patent leather shoes. I saw it all sliding together in a heap, melted, smoked and charred. We had been known on my street for having a brick house once, with a garage, an air conditioner, and the best birthday parties they'd ever seen.

I felt only curiosity as I used a stick to lift charred boards, my feet unsteady swinging over the spongy damp ashes and coarse burned things that made a dull scraping sound when my feet moved. I didn't feel the loss. I still had my Barbie and Ken safe in their shoebox home, so I didn't cry. I couldn't remember anything I had lost, didn't know even what to look for in the ruin.

*   *   *

My daddy slammed my mother's head again and again into a wall. He once beat her unconscious with the broken leg of a chair. Then he crawled over her, sucked at her crotch not seeing us there, not hearing, not knowing anything but what he wanted to do. We stared at the man sucking at our mother's crotch, too drunk to move the girdle off those heavy dead weight hips. I wondered why he was doing it. I saw the dull spots of blood stains on the white girdle where my mother's periods had caused accidents. I could hear her always asking me to watch for some stain on the back of her dress, knowing this blood was something shameful, but he didn't see it. Blind drunk, he lay between her legs and sucked until he gave up, took her blue high heel and for some reason decided to smash it in her head. I grabbed his wrist and screamed, "Daddy, don't do that!" I knew he would kill her, so I grabbed his arm, hung on and screamed. He turned and stared at me as if I had appeared suddenly from thin air. Then he crawled away.

How did I find the voice to say the words, to reach and grab my daddy's arm, to keep his hand from smashing the blue high heel into my mother's head? I found it somehow, and sometimes I still hear it pushing up at the back of my throat.

"There's no telling what that girl might say," they had said about me. They were amazed at the words I came up with and wondered how I'd picked up such a vocabulary, not realizing how well I always listened, not knowing my compulsion to find a quiet place, open a book, any book, and try out the words, feel them on my tongue and read. "She's smart as a whip," they'd say. "Lordy, you never know what that child might say."

A living doll is capable of anything. Not like

Shirley Temple who plays her lines from a script, not like a Chatty Kathy doll with her limit of recorded messages wound up behind a speaker in her chest, safe messages neatly coiled there to be released on demand with the pull of a string. Chatty Kathy's round freckled face kept smiling, her blue eyes with their stiff, glued-together lashes closed when you put her on her back, and unless you pulled her string, she wouldn't say a word. "Don't that feel good? Don't that feel good?" A dead doll of plastic blinks, nods, says nothing, but a living doll, she learns. There's no telling what a living doll might say.

I know what happens to a plastic doll when you bury it. I tried it once, then dug again, felt the hard nudge of my digging spoon against her cheek, saw the eyes sealed shut, then pulled her up and out. Only one eye opened. I threw her down, ran, and screamed. What happens to a plastic doll buried? Nothing. It comes back, hair matted, one eye open, pink-bow lips curled around teeth full of dirt. She'll last longer than a mortal life and look more monstrous with each burial and resurrection. Each revival requires a little more bathing, holding, and pressing into something that looks almost worth loving again. It takes more effort to keep her looking human. She keeps her eyes wide open, her pink-bow mouth partly open in a smile showing a hint of teeth that will never bite. Sometimes there is a hole punched in the center of her lips, ready to receive the hard plastic tiny tip of a tap-water bottle, or a toothpick, or dirt, or anything someone has a mind to try to cram in. She smiles no matter what she is fed, no matter how many times you bury her, smack her, twist her head off, tear her torso free from arms and legs. Death cannot touch that molded friendly open loving face, a doll, a sweet thing with the face of an angel. A living doll keeps smiling; for a living doll nothing can be dead.

*   *   *

I found a dead snake once, carried it home bent, limp, and black on a stick. I dropped it on the porch, hid it under an overturned cardboard box with a brick on top to keep the dogs away. Then I went inside and found one of my daddy's sharp pocket knives, one he used sometimes for gutting fish. I took it from his top drawer tackle box, not stopping this time to play with the red rubber worms, plastic minnows, lead weights, red and white bobbers, feathered hooks. I sat on the concrete slab of our porch, stretched the snake out and made a long cut down its gray-yellow belly. I cut through the tough finely-ridged skin, pulled it open with an old bent nail and dug out what I could find inside. Cause of death: unknown. It didn't seem to have been squashed or run over by a car. It only seemed asleep by the side of the road. I pulled out the black, gray and red strings of tissue inside. I tried to locate the heart, lungs, belly, but couldn't tell what was what, so I threw the rubbery stuff into the grass where something, a dog, cat, opossum, or skunk would surely eat it and drag it away.

I scraped the inside smooth with my knife-edge, listened to the soft dry rattle sound of metal grazing skin. I left the head on, couldn't see a way of gutting the head without crushing the shape of it, and I loved that thin black tight line of a mouth, the glass black bead eyes. I hoped it would dry without stinking, hoped there wouldn't be much in that paper-thin skull that could rot. I had heard that worms were just one long belly and figured it could be true of snake. I cut the guts out and hoped the brain would just shrivel and shrink to nothing more than a seed.

I ran the skin along my arms, hands, fingers, closed my eyes and felt the skin tickle across my neck and face. I wanted to slip inside that tight skin and wriggle through the grass to the woods and feed on bugs and berries— whatever snakes ate. I wanted to know the feel of living in snakeskin clothes and I thought maybe if I could find enough snakes, I could stitch the skins together and wear them, be supple and silent, yet still alive.

I curled the gutted snake around my wrist and liked the look of its smooth gray-black skin on my pale freckled arm. I tried knotting it together, but it wouldn't hold. So I slipped into the house and found scotch tape and then made myself a snakeskin bracelet, arranged the head to fall centered on the back of my hand. I was something wild then, exotic. I sneaked in the bathroom and put on lipstick, powder, and practiced drawing on black-lined Cleopatra eyes.

* * *

We lived in the country, had six dogs, "Baby," the mother German shepherd, married to her son "Bo" and their four puppies we had not been able to give away. But there were four kids so each of us claimed one until it was time to lose it, even then knowing that to own one was a temporary stage. My puppy was named Sybil because I'd read a story about Sybil, a beautiful witch, and the name seemed to fit her silver black coat. My Sybil had been missing for days. "Dogs roam," Momma kept saying. But she was only a puppy, I argued, and puppies were supposed to come home.

It happened every summer. There was a stench outside. The septic tank backed up, and Daddy had to lift the heavy lid, dip tools into the muck and clear whatever seemed to clog it when there wasn't enough rain. The tank was in the back yard, not far from the swing set, its lid like a roof on a playhouse. My mother had planted lush green mint around it. We often played there, mindless of the muck beneath. We enjoyed the elevated square of wood where we could play house, board games, Barbies, pretend to be on a raft bobbing down a wide river in the back yard. But sometimes it smelled awful, and Daddy would shake his head, frown, go outside and fix it the way daddies were supposed to do. "Don't play near that thing," Momma said when it was stinking. "It's nasty. You might pick up some kind of disease."

It was a Sunday morning, still cool, just after breakfast. My daddy said he'd have a look. He put on overalls, thick brown gloves, and took a shovel, rake, and a broken broomstick. I followed and watched, still not understanding the mysteries of toilets and septic tanks any more than I grasped electricity, radios, the tides, the order of planets and movement of stars.

Sally and I sat far back in the grass as he bent, gripped the lid in his hands, and pulled. I could see it was heavy. My daddy was a big man and had to lift it, take a breath, then slide the wooden platform sideways where it tilted into the grass. My sister and I covered our mouths and noses with our shirts. The stench was awful, and we stood way back because we'd been told the trap was deep and full of sewage—we might drown if we got too close and slipped.

His face was awful, twisted, frowning in the heat. I could see he was doing his best to get this finished without having to breathe. He stirred the thick gray muck with the broomstick, made a face, stepped back. I moved closer, knew he had found the problem and could solve it, but he hated the job. I could see by the way he clenched his jaw and turned his head. He saw us watching. "Y'all get inside," he said. But I wouldn't move. "Get on! You kids don't need to see this!" Those words only locked my determination, a forbidden sight from the sewer, I had to know. My little sister ran off, but I stood there and watched him bend to pick up the shovel, stoop and reach into the sludge and lift something, the sodden dead shape he had found. The thick muck dripped off in clumps, almost steaming in the sunlight as he swung the shovel, then dumped it all in the grass. "Go on!" he yelled.

But I went closer, saw it, the shape of Sybil there, my puppy, the flies already swarming, the mouth open, tongue gray and thick, stiff between her teeth. I couldn't stop staring. I stood, clenched my hands at my sides, and screamed.

How did it happen? How did a puppy get trapped in a septic tank covered with a lid that was difficult even for my daddy to lift? We looked for a sign that she had clawed her way in, drawn by the smell. Dogs are like that. Maybe she had dug a hole under the lid somehow and fell in. But there were no signs of digging. Momma said someone must have done it on purpose. Someone threw her in for meanness, someone's idea of a trick. I'd seen boys blow up frogs with firecrackers; I'd seen them club an opossum to a bloody mess for fun. I'd heard how easy it is to stomp mice, swallow goldfish, drown cats. I grasped what should have been beyond me. My Sybil was thrown in a sewer and drowned.

I never got the chance to bury her. Daddy said he would take care of it, but from the window I saw him load the trash can and carry my Sybil off to the dump.

I laughed at death once. Not long after the death of Sybil, I learned the tool of irony, distance, humor, how to take off from pain. It was my goldfish: Flip and Flap. I was cleaning out their fishbowl, standing at the kitchen sink, my mom peeling potatoes alongside me at the counter. I used a ladle to scoop the fish out, put them in a fresh bowl of water while I used a rag to scrub their bowl, wipe the scum off the glass, arrange little rocks and seashells at the bottom. I wanted them to be happy, and dutiful as always, I took care of my pets. But this time for some reason I was hurried, felt the pressure of something over or behind me. I was nervous, felt the ground trembling under my feet, and in my confusion I switched Flip and Flap from bowl to bowl, cleaning each bowl out, and then poured them down the drain. I saw the bright flashing tails sloshing down the dark hole in an instant. I gasped, saw them in my mind again, spilling and splashing with water down the drain.

"What happened?" Momma said.

"They're gone," I whispered. I glanced at her, then looked from bowl to bowl to be sure of their absence. I bent and stared down the drain as if somehow they might throw themselves up again into the air. I'd seen it at the lake; sometimes fish threw themselves out of the water. But not Flip and Flap. "They're gone," I said again. "I poured them down the drain." Suddenly I was laughing. I held on to the rim of the sink. "Flip and Flap are gone." I could see them together in the dark tunnel of water, looking puzzled at each other like cartoon fish. I could see them gush from pipe to pipe to the Tennessee River, see Flip and Flap, yellow cartoon characters beyond death in animation, flapping their fins and talking to each other as they found their way out to sea. I couldn't stop laughing. Then I was crying, laughing, and crying until my mother pulled me to a chair, held me and said, "Don't worry baby, we'll get you more," as if that could bring them back.

*   *   *

My friend April lived beyond the small patch of woods across from my house. When her dog Joe died, she immediately came panting red-faced, out of breath to me. "We gotta bury Joe," she said. She didn't tell me how he died, just that we had to bury him, and she stood there waiting for me to tell her what to do. The problem was he was a big dog, part golden retriever maybe, some German shepherd mixed with something else. He weighed as much as I did, at least. She said she wanted to start her own cemetery in her back yard and since I had my own tiny graveyard for my pets, I had to come and help her pick the spot.

I took Daddy's shovel and a yardstick, and I ran inside to get the small white leather New Testament that had been given to me at vacation Bible school. I knew I was to read "ashes to ashes, dust to dust," but I'd never find the phrase in all those words, so we would say what we knew of the traditional ceremony and grip little Bibles in our pious, sweaty hands.

As we entered her back yard she told me, "Joe looks awful." I stopped and stared over at the heap wrapped in an old red blanket in the corner of her yard.

"Let's just do it," I said. I found a spot where the dirt looked soft under saplings, so we cleared leaves and started to dig. The heat was thick with gnats, flies, mosquitoes, bees. April wanted to wait until it got cooler. I frowned at the dirt and kept digging, said, "He'll only stink, April. And the flies will get him. How would you like flies crawling all over you?"

We dug silently until the hole looked huge. It was late, and we were hot and hungry. "It's supposed to be six feet for humans," I said, "and half that, three feet for a dog," as if there were a formula for the way these things were done. We pushed, pulled, and prodded old Joe over, rolled him into the hole, and covered him quickly. But the hole wasn't deep enough. There was one blond paw still sticking out. We piled on more dirt, tried adding rocks and leaves, but I knew it wouldn't work. Finally I stepped back wanting to cry from the sheer heat and dirt of it. "We've got to pull him out again," I said.

April stepped back, turned toward her house, plopped on the ground, and said. "We've got some peanuts and lemonade in my house." She stood and without a word I followed. We washed our hands and faces, stuffed ourselves, and watched Popeye cartoons on TV until her dad came home. We told him the story, and I felt like crying with relief when he said, "That's all right, girls. I'll do it. You go on and play."

What a daddy, I thought, as we went to April's room to play grown-up with her momma's makeup. Her momma was snapping beans for supper, and her daddy was sitting at the kitchen table eating peanuts and drinking iced tea. It was quiet in her house. I watched April sit with cotton balls stuffed between her toes, painting her toenails cherry red. She wasn't worried about Joe. Her daddy would bury him; her daddy wouldn't take him to the dump. All she had to think about was perfectly painted toes. I turned to the mirror and looked at myself, forced a smile to show my dimples, then turned my profile, lifting my chin, and tried a sultry look. No use. I still had a baby face, even though I'd made my mother cut off those Shirley Temple curls. I wanted a new look. I was ten, almost a grown-up. Some girls in my class were already wearing bras, though I still had the wiry thin body of a boy. I picked up a black eyeliner pencil, touched the tip with my tongue, and pulled at the corner of my eye.

I practiced again and again, erasing the mistakes with Vaseline, worked until I had it. I stepped back to see myself, sucked in my cheeks, trying to show cheekbones. My mouth looked like a fish, and my hair was stringy from sweat and dust, but I had it. I turned to April, did my best to tilt my head in a regal pose. "Look, I've got Cleopatra eyes."

* * *

"Count your blessings," my momma always said. "Be grateful for what you've got."

One Christmas I got an Annie the Accident Doll. It was a cheap Christmas, a desperate Christmas, a struggle to act out the required drama of peace and good will. We knew our toys came from the "Toys for Tots Drive." Annie the Accident Doll came in a torn white cardboard box with a red cross stamped on the front. She came with accessories that could only sicken, hurt, or heal: A thermometer painted with a red line permanently fixed at 102 degrees, a pink plastic crutch that fit in her slotted pink hand and under her arm, a bloody gauze bandage to tie around her head, a sling for one arm that was jointed at the elbow to bend into the ready-made cast, and even stick-on pink circles for chicken pox or measles, whatever disease I desired. She was a stiff sad thing in a pink dress, her panties missing along with the Band-aids and half of what would be her chicken pox scars. Her hair was tangled, dress rumpled from some other little girl's hands. Clearly a used thing, her hair would never go back right again, and one glass eye kept sticking shut.

It was a day of tangerines, candy canes, dirty stuffed animals, used sweaters, cars with wobbling wheels, bent Slinkeys, tangled yo-yo's, old things one step away from someone else's trash. There was one new toy, a red plastic fireman's hat for Glenn. He was proud of that hat, ran around the house with a detergent bottle ready to squirt and extinguish an imaginary fire. My daddy grabbed him, a long arm swung out from the chair where he sprawled, dozing, or cussing, drooling, chewing his dead wet cigar, crying, yelling, head shaking, a pathetic stinking drunk. His hand reached, caught Glenn around the waist, grabbed the fireman's hat and flung it, plastic crashing with a smack against the wall. Glenn scooped it up and, silently crying, stood there and punched the dents back out to some kind of shape. I stared at this man I called my daddy. He glared at Glenn and said, "Throw it out, god-damn it. You don't want to be a fireman like your daddy. Your daddy is sorry as hell. He's no damn good." Then he leaned forward and sobbed.

There was no room for anger, rage, no defense against my daddy drunk and crying on Christmas. I was the used doll, newly wrapped and unwrapped only to comfort, listen, staring blankly as he clutched and mashed me against his sweating chest. I was a doll who did what the man at the factory had made me do.

I listened for my mother, prayed she'd stay in the kitchen, drinking from her own hidden bottle of bourbon as she mashed and tore white dough canned biscuits for chicken and dumplings, her homemade Christmas specialty.

I was Annie the Accident Doll, the broken thing with dirty red hair and lost panties. I came equipped with a fixed blank mouth and eyes, uncomplaining, and ready to survive all kinds of pain.

I burned that doll that Christmas. I gave her all available diseases and accidents in a single day, then carried her out to the trash. I burned her in the barrel, watched her face blacken and melt, saw her pink dress shrivel and burn. I was Chatty Kathy locked away in a closet, shaking my head, shouting into the darkness, my silent voice crying, "No! No! No!"

* * *

I used to shave my heels in the bathtub after a long soak in hot water, using my mother's razor. I liked to watch the dead white skin clump up the blade, shake it clean in hot water, and shave the balls of my feet, toes, ankles, legs. I even shaved my arms. Had I been old enough for pubic hair, no doubt I would have shaved that too, aiming for the clean bare folds of skin as pink and white as the plastic bottom of a doll.

I bit my nails, chewed my hair, plucked out my eyelashes, peeled my lips with my teeth, tore scabs just to see the bright bursting drop of blood. I was alive if I was bleeding. Anyone knew that only girls, not dolls, could bleed.

"Ignore her, and she'll quit," Momma said. But I kept at it, ripping at myself, blind and indifferent to whether I was noticed. I drew back into my own secret closet inside where I could do what I wanted, clicking and whirring out my mechanical habits until a gear snapped, a wire loosened, a battery sealed tightly in my back ran down. I stopped in time, a dead thing, a doll worn down who only stood still, opened her eyes when they raised her, waited for her arms and legs to be moved.

* * *

"Whore slut bitch cunt. You goddamned no good cocksuckin' whore." Words I knew before I knew them. Slap-sound words pounded my ears. I stood back, held the wall behind me, listened, watched, not knowing what the words meant, but knowing by the way he spit them out that they were something awful like the cat pissing on the couch, the puppy shitting in the hallway, something awful, disgusting and mean. My mother stood there, face blank, shaking the ice in her drink, staring at him defiantly, sometimes whispering, "You son of a bitch." Words slapped, wrestled, grabbed, and clawed until finally he exploded across the room, grabbed her with one hand and slapped, punched, shook, slapped again, until she screamed, "Please! Stop it! Please!"

What was a whore, I wondered, knowing somehow it was a bad woman, something dirty, like a bug or a rat, something rotten and sneaky and mean. My mother was one some-

68

times, according to Daddy. Even my sister, Ruby, was one, he said. And he fucked whores sometimes. He'd tell us. He'd come in drunk and tell how he fucked whores, and he said it with a grin. He puffed up his chest, and shot the words out with pride, as if he had hit a moving target or caught a monster fish. He would come in drunk and dirty, swagger across the kitchen and throw a beer bottle at my mother. "Yeah," he'd sneer. "God damn it, I went out and fucked me a nigger blond whore!"

I tried to see this, but couldn't. I saw images of black women like the ones in his magazines, women with giant round breasts, long legs spread. Some had straight black hair; some had Afros; and some with those white-blond bubble hairdo wigs. I'd seen the magazines he kept under the mattress on his side of the bed. My sister had shown me. "That's what happens when you grow up," she said. I saw the white woman laid out on a table with fruits piled all around her and between her legs, the men with their clothes on bent over eating, one licking cream off her belly and one reaching for a grape from the cluster between her legs with his teeth. She looked dead to me, and I knew she was a whore. I cried and told

Ruby that I was a good girl and that would never happen to me. But I couldn't stop looking at the dead whore woman being eaten like fruit. Her eyes were closed, arms at her sides, her palms turned up empty to the air. The men crowded around her like our dogs at feeding time when I scraped kitchen scraps into pans scattered in the back yard. The bad-girl-whore-dead-woman lay there, in the black and white photograph, her blond hair sprayed into a flip just above her shoulders, her eyes—I looked closely, they were shaped with black liner, and her darkly painted lips were slightly open as if she were about to kiss the air. She lay still, waiting, and Ruby would never answer when I'd ask, "What happens after the picture. Will she wake up? What are they going to do?"

I'd never be like that. I was a good girl, just like Shirley Temple. I'd never show my bottom to anyone my except the doctor and my mom. "Keep your knees together like little ladies," Momma said. "It isn't nice to show your underwear." Sometimes I'd ask "What about Shirley Temple?" and she'd snap, "That's the movies, now you just shut your mouth and do like I say."

She had us trained to respond to the snap of her fingers, a snap that cracked like a whip

to my ears. I see her still snapping and cross-
ing her middle finger over the index finger as
signal for us to put our knees together,
straighten up and sit like good little girls. She
said, "I won't have people thinking my girls
are trash."

I learned posture by being forced to pace the
living room with an encyclopedia on my head.
I liked "D" best, because it wasn't too thick,
and I loved to flip through it and study the
pictures of dogs, famous dams, and the illus-
trated history of dolls. I remember the weight
of the book balanced on my head, tilting and
sliding off when I giggled, the relief and praise
when I made it across the room without it falling down. I was the best of all of us. I practiced.
I took a book on ballet from the library and
studied posture. I learned to bend my knees,
raise my arms, lift my legs without moving my
head. I could be a ballerina like the twirling
plastic figure in my musical jewelry box. I
wanted to be in her pink painted-on outfit,
wear the tiny crumbled piece of netting that
was her tutu. When I opened the box, she
would bounce up on a little spring attached to
her feet, and if wound would twirl balanced
on her long pink legs in front of the small
diamond-shaped mirror glued against the lid.

My ballerina would never bleed like my

mother. I studied her smooth molded plastic skin. Her legs were sealed shut. She would never bleed like my mother who sat on the toilet, spread her legs and made a sour face as she took the soggy bloody pad from between them and unclipped it from the white elastic belt. Her face had a disgusted look as she wrapped the pad in toilet paper, and pushed it into the trash. I could smell it, the metal-sharp dirt smell of blood. "Why do you bleed like that?" I asked.

"Because a woman has to," she said.

"Does it hurt?"

She stood with the fresh pad hidden securely now between her legs, bent to the sink and washed her hands. "You get used to it," she said. "Like anything, you get used to it all."

I could hear my sister's words: "You don't want to grow up. It just gets worse every year." And I wondered if my sister bled too. Was that what made a whore? Blood between the legs? I knew it was bad, could see that from the look on my mother's face as she shoved that soggy stinking tissue-wrapped pad deep into the trash. Already I was embarrassed for something I didn't own yet, dirty, leaking blood. Already I was trained and ashamed.

I liked to help my mother clean. I would dust the end tables, dry the tableware, arrange, re-arrange it all neatly in the drawer. I liked things neat. Daily I would wipe my shoes and slip them back in the shoebox the way I tucked my baby dolls into their cardboard beds. I liked to help do laundry and would stand over the open dryer door, breathe the clean smell, close my eyes to the warm soft heat as I reached in and grabbed the thick terry cloth towels. I held them close as I carried them to the kitchen ta-ble where I would fold them neatly, getting the corners straight, breathing the smell, feeling the warmth as it spread and vanished into the cooler air.

As my mother sorted dirty laundry from the hamper, I tried to hold my breath against the sour smell of bath towels, damp socks, the oily dirt and cigar smell of my daddy's clothes. I crouched on the floor just to be near my mother. Waiting, I mashed soap powder be-tween my hands and rubbed the soft oily feel of it into my skin.

Once I heard her gasp, and I looked up to see her staring at my daddy's undershorts in her hands. I saw soft wrinkled fabric, the faded blue line print running up. My daddy's shorts.

He had lots of pairs like these. I had folded and put them away in his drawer many times before. She looked as if he had hit her. Then I saw that blank dead look she took on whenever he yelled at her: ""Bitch, slut, whore." I stood and saw that she was staring at dried, red-brown smears on the fabric where he opened his shorts, pulled apart the snaps. She was crying. She wadded up the fabric and whispered, "You son of a bitch!"

"What?" I said reaching.

She yanked them away and yelled, "Don't touch that!" She yelled in that same voice she used once when I found a dead rat in our back yard.

"Your daddy is a bastard," she said, as if I knew what the word meant. I hugged her thigh and wanted her to hold me. She glared. I wanted to run but was afraid to be alone. I stepped back, put my hand on the cold green metal of the dryer and watched her grinding my daddy's shorts between her fists, her teeth clenched.

"What's wrong with daddy's shorts?" I said, knowing it was blood. I had seen the way dried blood looks on dish towels. I bit my lip to stop the trembling and asked, "Why don't you tell me what it is?"

"It's blood," she said, suddenly cool and calm as if she were telling me that it was raining, and that was why I couldn't go out and play.

"What happened to Daddy?" I asked.

She stared at the smear on the cloth as I watched her face and saw her slip away, knowing that I was alone. Then suddenly her voice came deep and slow, distant like an echo from the bottom of a well. "It's some whore's blood," she said. "Your daddy was screwing some whore, and he didn't bother to take off his shorts."

"Did it hurt?" I said. It made sense that when a man stuck his thing inside a woman she would bleed.

"I wish it did," she growled. "I hope his god-damned cock rots off." She threw the shorts on the floor and stomped at them again and again as if killing a snake that wouldn't die.

I covered my mouth with my hands and ran out the kitchen, down the steps, and outside. I ran through the rain, went to the edge of the yard, crouched and hid there under the hedge. I stared at my house as if any minute a monster would come roaring out, something huge and bloody and screaming, foaming at the mouth. I pressed my hands into the cool grass, dug into the black dirt, and yanked up fists full of grass. I buried my nose in the fresh wet smell of things growing, rain, earth, grass, life.

* * *

Some days I refused to wear dresses fearing that someone would catch a glimpse of my panties under all those crinolines, that starched stiff skirt. Some days I refused to wear pants or shorts, seeing in the mirror the curve of my butt, the words ringing in my head every time I walked away from a grownup, hearing a little laugh, "Look at that butt, look at that cute little round butt, got a butt like a peach, a little ripe peach." I could hear Daddy Gene's joke and the men all snickering: "You know why a woman's like a peach?" I didn't get the answer, something about round and furry and juicy. I wouldn't eat peaches after that. My sister was right. Life was getting harder, dirty, sneaky, and mean.

But I was still the good girl, more frightened of my daddy than ever because I knew his secret. He had stuck his thing inside a whore and made her bleed. At night in the dark I'd slip my hand in my panties and feel the soft folds of my skin. At any sign of moisture, sweat, any sign of dampness, I would throw off the covers and run to the bathroom, peer between my legs, and see if I was bleeding. My mother had said all women bleed, and in my mind, when you bled you were a whore. I wanted to be my little plastic ballerina, wanted my legs to be pink plastic, molded together forever. My ballerina would never bleed.

So I worked to stay the good girl. I didn't eat much, never argued, mopped the floors and used my spare time to clean rocks and sticks from the yard. If I couldn't say anything nice, I wouldn't say anything at all.

It worked. My daddy never hit me. I was the good girl, the one he'd come to crying after his fits of beating, breaking, his crazy storms of rage. He slammed the cat against the wall once for nudging his foot while he sat watching TV. His arm swooped, and he caught her, threw her smack into the wall. I heard the thump, watched it slide down to a heap on the floor, eyes staring, mouth open leaking a pool of dark blood soaking into the orange and white fur. I stood choking on my own trapped air. I couldn't scream, stood there gasping, head ringing, until it all faded as someone took me by the arm and pulled me away.

I was the bait used to soothe his savage

moods: "Shirley, go talk to him, go on, try to calm your daddy down." What would Shirley Temple do? I had seen her climb the steep path in *Heidi*, had seen her play, create a space for herself with straw and a blanket in that scary old man's house. She had kept beaming, oblivious to his rudeness, his roughness, his hostile stares. She walked straight to him, smiling, believing sincerely that since he was her grandfather, he must be good. She wouldn't see the danger and had no other options. She was orphaned. She couldn't go back down the mountain alone.

The man I called my daddy sat leaning against the table, sad and broken as he looked at his workboots, the stains on the wood floor, his calloused, black-nailed, oil-caked hands. He felt me come toward him, looked up, crying as he reached for me and shook his head. He always took his wallet, gave me all the money, twenties, tens, fives, singles. "You take this, baby," he'd say as he pushed the bills in my hand, "I'm sorry baby, sorry as hell." I could smell him, had to hug his neck, hold my breath against the stink of his cigars and whiskey, his awful, drunken, dirty sweaty smell. I squeezed the money in one hand, and felt my mother watching as I held my breath. Why me? Why did he always cry at the sight of me? Was I so like Shirley Temple that a glimpse of my sweet open face could flood a man in guilt? Maybe even a monster was capable of shame. "Go on, take it," he said, giving me the money, kissing my face, his mouth wet, slobbering on my lips, the rough stubble of his beard tearing at my skin. "I'm a sorry no-good bastard." I hugged him for as long as I had to, then ran crying, throwing the money at my mother as soon as I got out of the room.

I had once loved this man without effort, a stranger who took me in and raised me as his own girl. And he loved me. I gave love back and called him my daddy simply because he was there; but I was learning. Nothing came simple. Even love was something bought, something paid for.

When we needed groceries I was the tool. My mother planned it, snuck a penciled list in my pocket, told me to ask daddy if I could go with him when he went to the store. He'd bathe, shave, even throw on Old Spice sometimes, and we'd go to the big new grocery, not the Piggly Wiggly or the Buy-Rite, but the big one that had foreign things like Matzoh crackers and Chinese bean sprouts, Italian sausages and dried fish. He'd wave some new thing at me, baby corn, Greek olives, even a can of rattlesnake meat once. He'd offer, "You want this, Shirley? You want me to get this for you?"

If he knew how I feared him, it would have killed him. He looked so happy and proud, carrying those bags of groceries back out to the truck, with me following, popping caramel Sugar Babies into my mouth, unable to do anything but nod and smile, my teeth sticking together from the thick sweetness. He never knew I hated going, hated following his cigar, workboots and clean overalls. I was forced by my mother to go. She'd grab me on his paydays and say, "You ask him if you can go with him to the store. He won't say no to you, Shirley, he never says no to you."

"But I don't want to," I'd say. "I've got homework, I'm tired. I've got a headache. I don't want to go." I'd complain weakly, not really fighting because I knew any battle with my mother was lost.

She'd push me down the hall to go get ready, saying, "One day you'll learn to think of somebody besides yourself!"

But I loved him still for loving me, for buying me treats, showing me how to draw cartoon figures with quick free sweeps of a carpenter's pencil in his thick hand. He showed me card tricks, made me laugh by pushing out his dentures with his tongue, making them rattle; he'd do anything to get me laughing when he was sober. A good man or a bad man; I always knew by the smell of him. I could tell by the way the truck was parked in the driveway when I came in from school and could sense from a distance whether it would be a good day or a bad day. Possession. I'd seen it on *Oral Roberts*. I was sure demons hid in those whiskey bottles called Heaven Hill. Some days I wanted to call Oral Roberts, Mighty Mouse, Popeye, Jesus, Peter Pan, anybody to save us from my daddy when he was possessed.

I could have killed him one time. He asked me to, begged me crying to please shoot him so we'd all be better off.

My mother was in the bathroom washing blood from her mouth. Sally and Glenn had run out, and Ruby was already gone. I was there beside him because my mother had grabbed me, pulled me by the arm and forced me between them, said, "Shirley, stop him! Don't let him do this to me."

I was crying quietly, unable to look at my daddy, couldn't take my eyes off the painted splotched leather of his shoes. He dropped back, sank in a chair, then pulled the gun from his pocket, slid it across the table, and said, "Shoot me, honey. Goddamn it, you'd all be better off."

I stood there frozen and cried. He grabbed my arm and forced the gun into my hand. It wobbled heavily in my palm, the butt of the gun slipping on the wood of the table. I could smell, see the smear of Momma's blood on his hand and wanted to vomit. I hated him, but had to stop his crying, the tears from splashing on the table, had to stop his sniffing, sobbing gasps. It took both my hands to hold the gun steady. I felt the thick weight of it. He wanted to die, and I could kill him. "Just squeeze right there," he said. "It'll just take a second." He forced my hands to aim the gun at the center of his chest. "Just squeeze. You'll all be better off. Your daddy's no damn good."

I thought of it, imagined squeezing the trigger, the blast, his falling over, dead and silent and still. My mother would run from the bathroom yelling, "Shirley, what did you do?" And I'd say, "I did it." I would be a hero, but I would also be a killer, and would go to jail. I played over in my head all the times I wished he'd die on the way home in his truck, the times I prayed my momma would shoot him in a fight. I held the gun and wondered if they'd really put me in jail. My uncle, Daddy Gene, was a policeman, and he'd told me how they kill killers. He had shown me the handcuffs, let me feel the cutting click metal of them on my wrists. He'd shown me the guns, the police car with the back seat like a cage. They'd put me there for being bad. I'd be surrounded by policemen like Daddy Gene. He had taken me for a tour of the prison once, had shown me the dank concrete room where they kept the electric chair. I could see the wooden chair on the raised platform, the buckles and leather belts.

But he wanted me to shoot him, I would say. I'd tell them he wanted it. I'd cry and say I was only doing what my daddy told me to do. And it would all be over, like the times he'd finally passed out and the house was quiet and still. It could be like that always if I squeezed the trigger; quiet, peaceful, and still. If he had known how much I was tempted, he would have never given me that gun. He didn't know the rage of the girl who had sat in his lap, and looked so much like Shirley Temple, who colored pictures of her daddy flipping pancakes high in the air.

I threw the gun across the table and ran. I heard nothing as I tore through the kitchen, suddenly fearing he would shoot me now for not doing what he'd told me to do. I pushed open the screen door, ran down the steps, across the yard and into the woods and hid. I wanted to hide forever until someone could promise me, promise me and keep it, promise me that I was safe. Finally I heard my sisters calling from the yard, "Shirr-leey, Shirr——leey. He's gone. Come on back. He's gone now." I came to the edge of the woods and peeked out to see the empty driveway. I went in and helped my sisters heat beans and fry potatoes with onions for supper. Then we watched TV and ate cereal before we crawled under the covers and, dreading the sound of our daddy's truck, tried to find our way into sleep.

* * *

I walked home from school up a long hill on a tar and gravel road, past small brick houses, blocks arranged in a new suburb that grew around the school, past blackberry bushes, honeysuckle, woods where moss-covered rocks and saplings grew thick, woods full of copperheads, ring-necks, and king snakes. I saw two lizards once, clinging, wrestling, gripping each other with taut-muscled thighs and tiny claws. I thought they were fighting, and I stood watching until, feeling my presence, they scattered off into the woods and tumbled into the fallen leaves. Now, I know it was spring, already hot humid and thick, warm moist spring. They were mating, not fighting, some wild animal version of the act I grew up to call making love.

"God looks after drunks and little children," Momma always said. "But not enough," I'd say, breaking crayons for the smell of them, and scrawling mean, furious designs on my paper. "Count your blessings, Shirley," she'd say. "One day you'll learn to appreciate things." She'd show me pictures of starving children in Africa, the piled bony dead remains of concentration camps, people twisted and deformed from some mysterious disease. "Somebody's always got it worse than you," she'd say and I could never cry out, "But what about me?"

* * *

A doll's head can be filled with water if you drown her in the bathtub. You can squeeze her plastic cheeks together, make her squirt a stream of arcing water, splashing harmlessly into the air. You can drown a doll, then hold her up and watch her pee, see the clear water trickle from her hard round white belly through the precisely punched hole between her legs, watch the water trickle over her plump thigh and calves, see it drip from the curve of her feet to her plastic molded toes.

But a living doll chokes on water and dies if held under long enough. She struggles up for air, her belly, mouth, nose too full, too tight to smile. She fights back; crying, flailing against water, air, someone's muscled hands, eyes staring up at the overhead light. She cannot be pulled up, out of water, made clean, and revived.

My mother's hands once pushed me under water, and I went numb, looked up wide-eyed through the water, felt heavy and weighted by the dense liquid cloud above. I saw her white round face, her blue eyes dead while she seemed to be looking only at the water's surface. She couldn't see my face. I looked up at her dead eyes, felt the digging grip of her palms against my chest bones, her fingers, long pink fingernails digging into my shoulders holding me down. A doll-girl, I didn't fight, just wondered why this was happening. She was my mother and must have known about the danger underwater, must have known somehow that I was a doll, but still I was alive. My chest hurt; I shook my head, tried to get her attention, let her know I was underwater and if she didn't let me up soon I'd drown. I squirmed, but she only squeezed my shoulders harder. It hurt, and I didn't want my mother to hurt me, so I tried to lie still.

And then it hit. Possession. She was not my mother, but a demon. It had to be. My mother was possessed. I tried to call her back to the living world. I shook my head and squirmed. I tried to pull her from this spell, tried to scream: "Momma, it's me."

Finally over her shoulder I saw the darker shape of my daddy moving the way a mountain looms larger and clearer over the horizon as you drive. Suddenly she rolled, fell, was torn from me, and I rose up through the gray waves to the humid air. He grabbed her, pulled her up toward the rocky shoreline, and swung, her head rolling, snapping back with each smack of his fist. I watched and wondered whether her head would come off the way I'd torn heads loose from my dolls. I walked slowly up the shoreline, watching some strangers pull them apart. I heard screaming from a long distance. Then finally it was night, and somehow I was home.

* * *

"Look," Momma said when my Daddy kicked the bedroom door in. With a snap of metal, a crack of wood, we looked in to see her standing by the bed, shaking the ice in her drink, and holding a chip of plaster in her hand. "Look what I did." Then she turned back to the wall and loosened another chip of blue-painted plaster with her fingernail, pulled it loose, and widened the gray space of sheet-rock underneath the paint. She laughed and said again, "Look what I did." I stood looking at the bed and floor covered in plaster chips. The once-painted blue walls scarred, patches and trails of gray sheetrock gouged as if a monster had tried to claw its way out. My mother grinned and sipped her drink.

"You goddamned bitch," Daddy said, and walked away.

For once she had scared him. I thought he'd bolt across the room, and bang her head against the wall until she fell down dead. But the sight of her grinning, tearing at the wall, and calmly shaking the ice in her drink made him turn away. The truck started outside, and I heard him go. We walked in, drawn to her laughing, peeling at the wall like a devilish kid.

"Try it," she said. And it was easy. We used fingernail files, scissors, and combs from her dresser. Ruby stood on the bed to reach the high spots. Sally, Glenn, and I crouched on the floor to peel a wide gray river around the room, little streams branching off, a big gray river pushing forward and up to empty into Momma's ragged, chipped sea. We sensed the sun rising at the window, knowing that it was another day when we wouldn't have to go to school. My mother smelled like whiskey and sweat. Her fingers bled and her hands shook. I could see her cheeks sagging, puffy and pale, her lips fixed in that grin as she stared at the wall chipping away. I wouldn't go near her, but I worked at that wall just the way I dried dishes, folded clothes, swept the floor. This was another job, and I knew she would scream, smack, whip me with a belt if I dared say no. So we stood, sat on the floor, or leaned on the bed and kept peeling, knowing that once we had walked in the room there was no getting out until she decided to let us go.

Finally I stood, stepped back, and Momma glared. I smiled, waved my hand toward the wall, and said proudly, "It looks like a map of the world." Then I told all of them how the unchipped blue spaces could be hunks of land, showed them the little finger of Florida reaching down into the gray sheetrock sea. I pointed out what could be South America, Hawaii, Africa, Australia, and Japan. I had studied the map of the world in my school books and had tried to imagine what was going on in a single moment all over the earth: Crocodiles sunning on the river banks in Kenya, Eskimos running dogsleds across snowy fields, tigers hunting Indian villagers, monkeys swinging in South American trees. I looked at the torn walls of the room and tried to see all the possibilities in the world. I was tired and thirsty, my fingers sore. But I waited for my mother to let us leave.

Momma like to write on walls: phone numbers, messages, grocery lists, doodled hearts and circles, always curving flowering shapes winding around. The kitchen wall was yellow-painted paneling, thick with the grime of grease and smoke farther up toward a ceiling that darkened each year like a storm slowly moving in. But down by the counter was a history of messages, phone numbers without names, drawings, peace signs, dark-lined cat eyes, stick men and women, cats, bunny rabbits, boats, clouds, and suns. Everyone who used the phone had left a mark there. Like the walls of a public toilet, anyone could write anything that came to mind.

Our walls could tell you stories: the smack of plaster cracking, the crash of dishes, pots, bottles, a cat, a head, a shoulder, a fist. Anything gravity didn't lock in place could wind up smashed against the wall. There were bullet holes in most rooms, the smattering of buckshot scars on the dining room wall, a place in the living room behind a door where my mother shot a .22 and made a hole just large enough for me to stick my little finger through and feel the dark cool space behind. I could hide things there, tiny rolled-up messages, crumbs of bread, and the loose pills I'd found that had rolled across the floor from Momma's stash of drugs.

I hid things in the walls. I wrote secret messages on them behind the furniture, took a red marker and wrote, "I love you, your secret admirer," behind the chest of drawers. I wrote, "I love you, I love you, I love you," wherever no one else would think to look. I told myself fairies lived in the walls and they would help me when I needed them, but only when nothing else would work. I took care of my fairies, knowing nothing came from nothing, that even fairies gave only if you had something to give. I wrote them messages on tiny pieces of paper and pushed them through the holes. I dropped them cookie crumbs, tiny purple violets from the yard, crushed balls of aluminum foil, wrapping paper, tiny scraps of cloth. I knew my fairies would watch out for me if I took care of them, if I kept them secret and didn't tell.

I tried to forget that my own hand had written those love messages. I convinced myself sometimes that it was fairies that sneaked out in the dark and wrote me love notes in secret places. I told myself that in my dreams they showed me where to look when I needed to know that I was loved.

Everyone wants to run when they can't convince themselves that it's worthwhile to stay. Even Shirley Temple ran in *Our Little Girl*. And it was an act of defiance that lifted Dorothy out of Kansas, spun her in a black cloud and dropped her crashing safely to a foreign land, through a dark forest, along a yellow brick road to Oz. Huck Finn did it. Cinderella too. And Wendy led the others out the window to fly away with Peter Pan.

I was fourteen and had been sucked, poked and fingered more times than I could count. But I told myself I was still a virgin. When they pulled at me, tried to shove their tongues between my teeth, I held my mouth firm like the pearly-chip teeth of Chatty Kathy who resisted any penetration with that solid pink mouth. Like Chatty Kathy I spoke with my mouth tight, my voice prescribed sounds coming from some distant speaker in my belly. I was a dead thing with a pink-painted mouth, white chips for teeth sealed in, speaking only when the string was pulled, saying only what the factory man had programmed me to say.

"Don't that feel good?"

Every other night was a party at Momma's house. Daddy worked those nights at the firehouse—planning, I figured, how the next night home he would beat her for her boyfriends, plotting how for every night of her parties without him, he'd give her one night of revenge.

One day, I told a boy I hated my life. He told me he loved me, wanted to kiss me, said he wanted to be my friend. But I turned away and said I loved everyone in a spiritual way. I told him not to touch me because I was dead. He offered to take me home to his mother and said she'd adopt me because she was a good Christian woman and she would take me in.

So I brought my sister Sally who was eleven, with the boys already smooching at her, stroking her butt when she walked by. She knew what was coming. She'd seen the wrestling in the bunk beds, she'd seen the breasts, butts, and cocks bouncing naked down the hall on the party nights. She wanted to run too. My mother didn't notice when we walked out to my friend's car with a change of clothes and our toothbrushes in brown paper bags.

His mother stared at us from her kitchen table with the "Serenity Prayer" plaque hanging, painted white hands sweetly praying, on the wall. I knew she'd never play mother to us, not with that pink pantsuit, her hair sprayed tight as a helmet, and those lines around her mouth fixed in a straight thin line. "Take them downstairs," she said. She gave us apples, milk and cookies on a blue plastic tray, and said, "Take them downstairs, Randall. We have to talk about this."

So we sat in the finished basement, a small room with brown carpet, brown paneling, and the color TV with game shows turned on. We waited wondering, and when we looked up to footsteps on the stairway, I couldn't see beyond the policeman's uniform, his black leather holster, gun, nightstick, the gleaming badge.

It was my first ride in the back of a police car. I saw no door handles; I couldn't roll down the window; I was locked behind a wire screen, with the heater cranked high, the air thick and dry. I squeezed Sally's hand on the car seat beside me. I couldn't look at her, but knew she was crying. I stared out the window at the cars going where they wanted, the people walking down the sidewalk, waiting to cross a corner. They smoked cigarettes, held newspapers, carried purses, briefcases, had a life.

Downtown near the police station, the courthouse, post office, the official business part of town, I knew he would arrest us, detain us, lock us in jail. We were caught, dumb as dogs about what would happen next. When he parked near the dog pound, I wondered if this was where they took runaway girls too; feared that they would gas us the way they did dogs that nobody claimed.

He led us up the sidewalk without a word, pressed a buzzer, and looked past the curtained glass door behind wrought iron bars. I stared at the brown concrete between my feet, felt Sally's hand sweating in mine, couldn't look up, couldn't ask a question, a doll again that did nothing, simply waited to be placed where someone wanted her to go.

A big gray-haired woman opened the door, looked at the policeman and said, "Bring them in," as if we were blind, deaf, and dumb things. I looked up, read the plaque by the door as we entered: Chambliss Children's Home. A jail for children, a Christian prison they called a home.

In the foyer, the woman squinted down at us and ran her hands over our heads. She turned to the policeman and said, "They look clean." She led the way, walking ahead, whispered with the policeman, exchanging and signing papers, her face locked, it seemed, in a permanent frown. "Come on," she said to us finally as she walked up the stairs.

In *The Little Princess* Shirley Temple was banished to an attic servant's room when orphaned. She had to clean, be polite to everyone, build fires in other girls' rooms, carry and shovel buckets of coal. She did it, only cried once alone in her room, and she was saved in time by a foreign stranger who brought gifts as she slept. I was Shirley Temple. I kept my head down, stayed polite, pasted a smile on my face and turned to Sally, squeezed her hand and said, "Don't worry. It will be all right."

The woman took us to a room, a big closet with shelves of shirts, pants, socks, shoes, and a rack of dresses along one wall. She gave us each a paper bag, and told us to take off all our clothes. "I'll give you new ones," she said, not wanting an argument as she turned and grabbed up an armful of underwear, socks, and nightgowns. I watched the flab of her arm shake as she quickly went through the dresses on hangers above our heads. She yanked two off, held them in front of us to gauge the fit, then shoved it all at us, saying, "Hurry up and put these on." We stared at her, standing in our underwear. "All of it," she said. "It's the rules. Don't worry. When you leave you'll get your clothes back."

I swallowed and held onto those words: "When you leave." We would leave. It wouldn't last forever. But when? I looked at Sally chewing her lip and nodded. We bent to pull down our underwear and put on the ones the lady had shoved in our hands. She led us down a hallway, opened a door with a key, and prodded me in, saying, "This is your room." Then without a word she led Sally away.

That night, sealed up, locked tight in my room, I sat on the floor and stared up out of the thick wire-screened window, watching the humming bright white streetlight outside. I squinted my eyes to lose focus and told myself it was the moon. I was a prisoner locked in a tower, sentenced to die for some brave act, and I was sending my prayer to the moon.

But I couldn't think for the yelping and howling of the caged dogs at the pound next door. I could see them talking to each other in dog voices, sending messages unknown to human ears, calling for help like those cartoon dogs in the movies. I knew that if I were in a movie it would be all right, someone would magically help us, we would be happy, playful as 101 Dalmatians, and we would be safe.

In the courtroom, our parents wouldn't look at us. I watched them, pale and yellow-looking in the hard light. They stared out at nothing as they sat next to what had to be a social worker with those pink lips, black pumps, navy suit, and sprayed hair. I sucked air in gulps to keep from crying, gripped the wooden bench beneath me to keep from running away. Finally they stood, and the judge shouted at them. He told them they would lose us for good if this happened again. He said that he was disgusted, that they ought to be ashamed.

We all rode home in silence, Sally and I staring out our windows, Daddy driving, viciously sucking his fat brown cigar. Momma stared straight ahead. I looked up at her blue-black hair and wanted to throw my arms around her neck, hug her just to breathe in her realness, her familiar smell. But I feared she'd slap me. I felt even in the back seat the threat of a hand raised.

I'd never run away again. I would take anything they gave me. I'd never run away to be locked up next to howling dogs. Never. I would go through anything to be near them, let them rip my head off, drown me in the tub, make me squirt water, watch me pee. I'd do anything, take anything. Nowhere else would I find a mother and a man to call my daddy. Anything was better than being abandoned, locked up like a lost dog, alone.

*   *   *

The truth of my real daddy came with flashing scissors. I was fifteen, shocked and ashamed of the way my mother had used a young black lover to run my daddy—the one I called my daddy—out. He did it with a baseball bat. He told my daddy that my mother was a mother and that nobody should hit a mother. I had never thought of that. I wondered if a man could hit a woman if she wasn't a mother, the way a man could eat a girl if she weren't a girl but a little doll instead?

Her lover never hit her, but he didn't need to. Once in place, he took power like some great daddy-man-king. She did anything he wanted. He didn't need to hit. He was my mother's savior, the first good man she said she'd ever known. But I knew better. I saw the savior become a sneak. I'd seen him selling her pot, making deals in the back yard, then come in, kiss her, tease her, love her up as he asked for money to buy cigarettes, beer, and gas. I wondered if Momma was cursed to make men who once loved her turn mean. They all did it. I watched her for some sign to show me that it was something she did.

100

Ronnie moved my mother out of her old bedroom. He said he hated sleeping with those scratched up walls. So they slept on the fold-out couch, the mattress permanently un-folded, covers tossed from their screwing, their teasing, their fighting, their sleep. We had to be careful in the morning not to see them do-ing it in the living room as we went to the kitchen to find something to eat. We listened, stood in the hallway, and waited for the thrust-ing and groaning sighs to die.

He didn't mind walking around the house naked, dangling his penis, eyes grinning, proud. He and my mother opened the house for parties, "socials," he called them, group highs. The music was Marvin Gaye, The Temp-tations, Issac Hayes. The drugs: Marijuana. Malt liquor. Cherry vodka. Gin. High school boys grabbed me in the hall, wet mouths press-ing, tongues pushing, hands prying into my clothes. "Don't you like black boys?"

"That's not the point, that's not the point," I said. "I don't like anybody. That's not the point!"

Once I screamed at my mother that she didn't act like one, that she was high all the time, and was sleeping with a man half her age. "It isn't right, you don't act like a mother at all," I said. Then she came at me with scissors, flashing silver sewing scissors ripping the air with her hand. Eyes cold, mouth twisted, she reached, swiped, and jabbed at the air. I ran to my room, scrambled up and crouched in the corner of my bunk bed where I swung the guard rail like a weapon, my mother's words stinging: "You little bitch, you piece of white trash shit, who the hell do you think you are?"

It was then she told me my legal daddy wasn't my daddy, not the man I called my daddy either. She said I was a bastard, no better than white trash, a goddamned little bastard bitch. She screamed at me, scissors jabbing until Ronnie came, and glaring at me, pulled her off and took her away in the car. I watched them back out the driveway. I could hear her voice still screaming: "You don't know shit, you little bastard. You don't even know who your daddy is!"

My daddy was a man I'd never heard of, a man who came in between the two daddies I knew. He didn't know me. He just knew that he made me, passed me on, sealed me up in a box on a shelf somewhere, and moved on. Momma said I had eyes like him, that I looked like him. I studied myself in the mirror, looked into my eyes for a sign of the man who made me, but found nothing. I only saw a freckled round-faced girl with a little mouth and big eyes looking back. I only looked like myself.

*   *   *

III

"Damn, Shirley, the least you can do is move," he said. My boyfriend got up from the bed, walked to the bathroom, and shut the door. He turned on the shower—I thought he wanted to wash me off his skin, my clinging sweat, that clear bitter salt rotten fish smell of me. I turned over, bit the corner of my pillow, shook, and breathed to release the clenched knot in my chest. I kept my face down buried under the quilt, stuffed the corner of the pillow into my mouth to keep from screaming. I held the pillow, shook with the choked noise, pulse of blood and air in my throat, and cried.

Move, move, move.

My baby dolls gave their heads up easily, just a squeeze and a twist and a pull and snap; the head would roll free, and I could peer in, breathe the new clean plastic smell inside, the hollow pink space like a pearly cave beyond the stiff plastic hole. I turned their heads over, looked inside where the hair was stitched into neat lines, and wondered if my hair grew like that in a tightly woven symmetry, perfect neat rows. I propped their heads on my finger, made them bob and talk, draped my finger in my daddy's handkerchief and poked it in their necks, waved them around like decapitated ghosts. Given a new doll I always looked inside their sheer white panties to see the pee-hole, the bare rounded butt, then ripped their heads off to look inside.

"The least you can do is move."

I tried, but my legs were stiff, squeezed together tight as the molded plastic ballerina in my musical jewelry box, my body still insisting that I was still a virgin if I didn't want him to put it in.

He was my boyfriend, the one I chose, the first I ever wanted. At fifteen finally I wanted someone for me. But still I went dead as he rubbed me. I was a pork chop being seasoned for the grill. Move, move, move. I could only lie there dead and wait for him to get it over and go away.

I had let the others do things, finger, push and probe, knowing that as long as they didn't put "It" inside me, I'd stay a virgin. I knew that "It" was the difference between whore and virgin, didn't know the proper word for "It" yet, just: weeny, ding dong, bone, cock, dick. But I knew "It" made babies, knew "It" made whores and blood, knew "It" hurt, poked at something deep inside you and made you bleed. And you'd never be a virgin again. If you wanted it and they did it, you would be a whore. If you didn't want it, God knew somehow and would keep you a virgin. Only a girl that wanted it could be a whore.

He was on me, over me, in me, tongue filling my mouth, breath hot on my face, fingers pulling, cock in, out, in, out, in. But he couldn't reach where I hid like a mouse inside the dark space deep inside beyond the reach of any finger, cock, tongue. I hid and watched his eyes clench, lips open, breathe. He thought he had me, but no one was there. Like the rest. They only thought they had me. I had let them lick and finger, rub me raw with whiskers, probe with their thick wet tongues. I had held my breath against the awful smell of them curling around me like a hard hairy fist. My own hands curled into fists at my sides as my knees tried to close, holding the knot inside.

They turned me over. I pressed my thighs tight, felt "It" hard and hot, poke between my legs as they moved me up and down. I was a rag polishing the leg of a chair, up, down, up, down, the wood glistening in the light. I stayed closed against them, as they whispered, panted, yes, yes. I pretended to sleep, and they let me, knowing I couldn't possibly sleep with them rubbing me raw like that, my chest pounding, ripped open like a chicken, breast bone pulled apart, the pink skin glistening before it is floured and fried golden brown in hot oil. I was a chicken: broken open, eaten, bloody, and raw.

"Ahh!" they cried out, squirted their hot juice across my skin, holding me against their chest in spasms. Finally they released me, went away, and let me lie there, panties pulled up again over my legs, rolled crooked, tight across my hips and waist. They left, and I was a virgin still.

"Damn, Shirley, move," my boyfriend said. I chewed on the pillow, crying, "I can't, I can't, I can't." I heard the shower's white hot noise, could see him naked in there, eyes closed in the steam, safe and deaf to me rocking, shuddering, stuffing my mouth with a pillow, and choking back the awful animal wrenching scream.

He thought I was a virgin, thought it worth a month of trying, coaxing with massage, oils, and wine. "Relax, relax," he said, but I couldn't shake the whisper, "Don't that feel good?" I held my breath, closed my eyes, focused, and pushed my thighs, vagina, hands, teeth all clenched tight as a fist.

He thought it worth the struggle, thought I was shy, nervous, and inexperienced. Fifteen and still a virgin he thought, so he was patient until it became such a habit that I got tired of fighting and he finally worked his way in. I let "it" in but still stayed locked up inside, shaking, hiding in the dark black hole of myself, receding farther back into my own cave. He came inside me, but no one was there.

He didn't know it was my daddy's whiskers, my uncle's fingers, all those hands of my mother's friends that pushed me back and held me. He didn't know it was the belt buckle clanking on the metal edge of the table rocking, creaking, grinding, into the wall that made me clench the sheet, the couch, the table to keep from drowning under the weight of so much skin, sweat, muscle and tongue.

"Damn, Shirley, the least you can do is move."

*   *   *

My boyfriend didn't know that I was thirteen when my mother first put a boy in my bed. He was thirteen too. Billy. A pretty boy, blue-eyed blonde, long limbs. At thirteen he lived as I did, on handouts from hippies, dealing what he could, abandoned by his mother, his father long gone. He smiled as I did, sweet with a soft voice, and those wide-open child's eyes. He is dead now. Died from an overdose of junk. He was on his way when I knew him. I knew his fear, his need to curl up in a tight fetal curl to sleep, hands and feet tight and covered in his effort to feel safe. They said, when he died at twenty-two, that he was skinnier than ever, teeth rotting, veins wasted, eyes burned out. "He was never a happy boy," they said, as if I didn't know. "He was just a kid." I cried, feeling more grief for this sad lost boy than I ever felt for myself.

He couldn't do it when they laughed and told him, "Do her, Billy, go on and do her," as if I were a new pill to be tried, a harmless psychedelic drug. "Go on, get in there and do her," someone said after my mother lifted my blanket and put him in. I could feel his skinny

109

body, cool skin. My mother had gone back out down the hallway, laughing somewhere, my mother who put this boy into my bed.

* * *

My top bunk bed had a narrow shelf of a headboard that still held my dolls, plastic legs spread wide to help them balance upright on the hard plastic curve of their butts, pee-holes covered by white nylon panties under flower-print dresses edged in lace. They sat, lined up in a row, blue eyes, all of them, staring into the dark. The bed shook with the movement of people fucking below me, grunting like bulls it seemed. I knew it was the biker, Frank, doing "It" to Ruby. I'd just seen him in the kitchen shooting up whiskey in his veins. I had seen his denim vest with a skull and crossbones on the back, his colors, the words "The Outlaws" stitched across his shoulders, had seen his scruffy red beard, long white arms covered in needle marks, shooting up whiskey in the kitchen because they'd run out of any better drug. And now he was doing Ruby, snorting like a pig in mud. She was fourteen and pant-ing the way she always panted when we raced across the yard. I listened, tried to tell if she liked it, but she only sounded hurried and out of breath.

I looked at Billy, saw the profile of him looking up at the ceiling. He was smiling, holding back a giggle, and I knew if the light were on, I would see him blush.

He moved a little closer, but I wasn't scared. He was skinny, skin smooth, face prettier than my face, only a boy. So we lay there, held hands in the dark and listened to the groaning underneath. Then I felt it. The familiar slide of fingers over my thigh, the smooth dip into panties, felt the bed shaking, heard the others grunting across the room, and knew what was next. I sucked in my breath and lay there, let him do what he knew he should. A hand rubbed my nipple while the other pulled my panties down, then he was on me, light as a leaf, a sheet, no heavy man this time. I lay still, thinking it was only a story as he moved over me, sucked my nipple like a baby, fumbled between my legs, pulled at himself trying to get hard. My dolls were shaking from the pounding below us, my books slid on the shelf, my rock collection rattled in the white cardboard box. I heard music from the living room, my mother's loud sneeze, and I knew they were sniffing Bactine from paper bags out there, falling back into a quick rush and bright visions. Sniffing Bactine always made my mother sneeze. I heard Ruby gasp beneath me. I wanted to look down to see if he was smothering her with a pillow. The sound was a hard sound like the breath knocked from Momma when Daddy knocked her down, but it was also light, like the sound she made when Ronnie was doing It to her on the couch in the morning when she thought we were asleep. I couldn't tell the difference. Pain or pleasure. All that grunting and gasping, strange and scary like the sound of rocks breaking, dirt falling, a wall coming down.

Billy sucked at my neck and tried to fit his thing inside me. He got my legs spread somehow but still couldn't get in. So he rubbed it back and forth against me, and I let him. I would still be a virgin. I was used to this. I chewed the inside of my lip and prayed he wouldn't get hard, wondered if a man had to have whiskers and stink with sweat before he got hard. I hoped I was safe, prayed I was safe since Billy was a boy. I knew he was a doll too, only doing what they had told him to do. But he did it. He finally squirted a few slick drops on my thigh, sighed, and moved over. He patted my face, then curled up tight next to me like a baby, and fell asleep.

I had an underground house. I found it with my girlfriends in the fifth grade, a square-shaped hole dug in the earth, four feet deep, with a sheet of tin over the top like a roof. We had discovered it one day walking through the woods, sneaked close to the sight of metal lid on the ground and listened. We feared it was a boys' club hideout, knowing even then it was a danger to get too close to a band of boys. So we stood there under the trees, looked at the tin roof, the clumps of leaves scattered over the sheet metal, the soft black dirt at the hole, the entry, where someone could come out, where we could go in. We stood listening, watching for a sign of danger, someone, something to emerge and attack. There was nothing but the dappled soft green of sunlight in the thick green leaves above, the light feathery whoosh of fallen brown leaves on the ground and wind in the trees. We went closer, crouched and peered in. I saw the bright shaft of light on the other side of the hole where the tin roof didn't quite reach. And in the dark shadows I saw an old mattress, a cement block, and I cautiously breathed the thick dank smell of dirt.

"Let's clean it out," I said, naturally the leader when it came to cleaning up buried things. Without a word they helped me lift and slide the metal roof. We held our breath, beat

113

the mattress with sticks to get the bugs out. Then we pulled, lifted it with sticks on one end to loosen cloth from dirt, pushed it and pulled, laughing and screeching at the thick scurry of bugs. Finally we tugged it out. I said we should make a bonfire and burn it once it dried. My daddy had told me a single un-watched cigarette could make a mattress burn. "Yeah," my friends said. We were girls who loved to burn things. On Saturdays we'd gather to light my family's trash at night, watching the sparks fly. For fun, sometimes we knotted plastic dry cleaning bags, tied them to hangers, and hung them from a tree to light and watch the burning plastic drop in yellow, blue-green, glopping plastic flames.

We claimed the hole and cleaned it out, swept it with whisk brushes pilfered from our parents, and took a tarpaulin to camouflage the tin roof. We worked daily, decorated the dirt walls with sticks, rocks, and weeds. We made plans one day to dig tunnels, expand and perfect our hole-in-the-ground home.

Then my friends grew up and into training bras, wanted to be cheerleaders, to be popular, and chase boys. I lost them the way we lose worn shoes. They just seemed to walk away.

So, as Billy curled like a baby beside me, sleeping peacefully, I slipped out, belly-slid over the side of the mattress, feet carefully reaching, balancing on the edge of the bed below me while the others slept. Once down, I pulled on jeans and a t-shirt, crept to the kitchen, grabbed a bottle of Coke, made a cheese sandwich, and slipped out. I ran quickly, softly as any wild scared thing. I ran into the woods, slipped through the trees, and took my shortcut to my secret home.

I sat, ran my palm over the crumbling dirt wall, and remembered how as a girl I stole the little broom and swept those dirt walls and floor clean. I had smoothed the edges and corners with a butter knife, arranged pretty rocks, filled empty Coke bottles with dried weeds. I had made a table out of taped-together shoeboxes and seat cushions out of plastic bags stuffed with leaves. It had become my house. My friends had forgotten it, busy with slumber parties and roller skating while my mother's house filled with strangers drifting in and piling up like dust in the corners.

I breathed the cool damp fertile smell of things growing, sweet with moss, leaves, and worms: a smell of fresh decay. I sat eating my sandwich, sipping my Coke. I was all right; I was still a virgin. I would take a bath later, start all over. I was still Shirley and a virgin because nothing had happened, nothing had happened at all.

In time, again, my mother's hands lifted my blanket. "Here's a place you can sleep, Lloyd," she said. "Climb on in." She giggled and said, "Now you be good to my girl." He snickered, already reaching, whispered, "I'll be good, Momma, oh yes, I'll be good."

He was a biker like the one that got Ruby, rough hands, tattoos, and cigarettes. A skull and crossbones, "The Outlaws" stitched across the back of his jacket. No boy this time, something closer to a man. His hands had torn engines apart. I had seen him rev his Harley, digging up grass and dirt in our yard. I had dodged his hands that always squeezed my arm. "Hmm, tender, can't wait to get a bite of that." They'd all laugh when he grabbed me, tried to kiss my neck. "I'm gonna get you sometime," he said.

But it was my mother who put him in, my mother, eyes wild from some drug, hair in long braids. They called her Momma B and she laughed in the dark, lifted my blanket, said, "Go on Lloyd, get in."

I pressed myself to the sheet, tried to pull away without moving, and faked sleep. He put an arm around me, pulled me close without a word. I went stiff, and he kissed my neck, said, "Relax Shirley-girl." A lick at my neck. A whisper. "It'll feel good if you give in." The hand pulled at my thigh, a grip so tight it pinched. "Don't fight it, don't fight. Ain't no way in hell you gonna win."

I knew this from the times they had held me on the couch, blew marijuana smoke in my face to get me stoned the way they'd held our dog's jaws closed, blew smoke in her face, and laughed watching her run across the room. "You'll feel better if you don't fight it," they had said. My mother frowned when I'd resist. "Just do it, Shirley," she said. "You always were a damned little snob."

His mouth sucked at my neck, palm covered my bony chest, fingers twisted my nipple as if he could make it grow, open, and give him what he wanted. I heard the couple below me, another biker and a girl who had hitchhiked from Ohio, who kept saying she'd been at Kent State and seen the whole thing. I heard them gasping and grunting the way I'd heard it a hundred times before.

Lloyd pulled my legs apart with one hand,

and squeezing my face with the other, he sucked at my mouth as if I were an orange with a hole dug out for him. The girl below me panted, "Like that, like that, like that." Lloyd propped himself over me and said, "That's balling, baby. Think you can ball like that?" He rubbed until my skin burned. I was a table, and he was sanding me down. He bit at my stomach, licked, then spit on his fingers and pushed them in.

The bed shook and the room pulsed with the sounds of mouths lapping, skin slapping, men panting, crying out. "It's like flying," the girl below said. I heard that sobbing, panting sound that could have been laughing or crying or just hard breathing. I felt my arms stretched out beside me and told myself I had big metal wings, I was a plane flying, slicing the air like a knife. I'd read the story of the Wright brothers. They had made the fastest bicycles, and went on to leap from dunes and make cold heavy metal fly. They had started out with a bike shop. I could see them, Orville and Wilbur, bending over a bike turned upside down, belly up, gears exposed. They were spinning the pedals, watching the black chain jump. They were trying to find a way to make the machine light, knowing the lighter she was, the less re-

118

sistance, and the faster she'd go. I could see their backs bent over the bike, perfecting the machine. "Come on, come on, come on," Lloyd said pulling me with him, rocking me like a wooden horse, yanking me back and forth. I saw the black chain spinning, heard the whirring sound of metal beating air as the wind carried me down a long black road. He pedaled and pumped. My head filled with his clanking noise. I was a machine, clanking, whirring, flying down a long black road.

I ran back to my underground house with nothing but my jacket, fearing I'd wake them if I went to the kitchen to find something to eat. I knew someone could hear me, rustling for my breakfast. Someone could grab me, hold me down again. I told myself I'd live on nuts and berries like the bears, live on nectar like the fairies, live on nothing like the saints.

With the crisp smell of morning, the crunch and whoosh of leaves, I walked toward the dull gray tarp on the ground. I slid in the narrow opening that seemed bigger than before. I knew the roof had been moved as I ducked in and smelled the difference. Something burned my nostrils. I knew the strong sharp scent of glue. I saw the beer cans, the crushed brown paper bags, the flattened metal tubes. I panicked, scraped my head on the jagged metal as I rushed out, sure somehow that someone would grab me and pull me back down. I ran, felt someone chasing me, even though I knew it was morning, and no one would get me because no one was really there.

*   *   *

The walls had peeled, the ceiling warped, and the junk had piled up in my mother's old room. Magazines, clothes, a broken blender, the iron and ironing board never used, a vacuum cleaner caked with dust like a dead thing propped in the corner. The dresser was piled high with stacks of old bills, school papers, Christmas cards, a bowl of rubber bands, clumps of nails and screws, a box of S & H green stamps, hairbrushes thick with matted hair and dirt, black plastic Afro combs, and piles of newspapers. I pushed open the door, shoved hard against a paper bag that had fallen, spilling Coke and beer bottles across the floor. I remembered peeling the walls, then later finding colored chalk and drawing bright pictures on the gray plaster: pink peace signs and rainbows, a crooked warped attempt at a blue flying dove.

At one time my mother had slept there with my daddy and my brother, Glenn. I had always wondered how they could all sleep in that bed. But half the nights Daddy slept at the firehall, and most times when home, he fell asleep on the couch. It was her room; he had hardly lived there. He just brought home paychecks, groceries, and whiskey. He only lived there sometimes, the man with the loud truck, cigars, whiskey and an oily smelling collection of tools, knives, and guns.

I pushed the door open farther, the knob falling loose, broken, dead in my hand like the hard round head of my doll. I closed my hand over the cold metal shape of it, slid through the narrow opening, and went in.

I took my mother's room without asking, claimed it the way a mouse gnaws its space in a wall. I carried the garbage and junk outside to the trash barrel one piece at a time. I burned what I could and stored what wouldn't burn in the hole under the house where our dog once crawled to have her puppies, where my Sybil was born. No one noticed, and if they did, no one asked questions. They'd seen me crying in the yard, digging a little garden, planting seeds, sitting in the grass, leaning on a tree, staring up. They saw me cleaning the house like a wind-up doll, scrubbing woodwork, dusting, waxing the floor, crawling on my hands and knees in the yard to collect and throw out the broken sticks and stones. "Bad trip," they said, shaking their heads, thinking it was a strong hit of acid that had broken me down.

I used a big butcher knife to hold the door shut, wedged it between the door frame and the wall, then hid there, listening for the slightest push against the door. I watched the metal blade of the knife bend against the strain of someone's weight. I cringed, silent, hiding, until laughing or cussing, some new stranger gave up and walked away.

* * *

My mother jumped from a cliff once. Proving her youth, she jumped with the boys from a rock bluff into a lake, and she dropped like a stone. She held her nose and stepped off into the empty air. I saw her face squinched tight as she fell with everyone cheering, "Go, Momma go!" She went straight down, sleeveless summer shirt flapping up from the brown shorts that squeezed her white and fattening thighs, like a rock she splashed into the dark water, then finally surfaced gasping for air. She paddled toward the cliff, and they helped her out saying, "Not bad, Momma B." She took a bow, and I watched from a distance knowing she was crazy, knowing they thought she was just a fat old woman who'd do anything they told her to do if they only gave her a cheer, a whistle, any kind of attention, any kind of praise. I saw my mother standing on a counter, showing her panties and singing for a doughnut. I knew then she would never change.

Days later at the hospital the doctor said pressure from the leap and smack against the water had burst a cyst inside her kidney. She had a severe infection, they said, and if they got her stabilized, and if she got through surgery, and if there were no unforeseen complications, she'd live.

A Christian group took me in, a self-made group that hung out in parks to testify and sing. They gave out free sandwiches sometimes, now and then baptized new members right out in front of everyone in the lake. I let them do it, let them put me in a man's white t-shirt, lead me over the grass, rocks, mud shoreline, let the preacher grip my hand and lead me into that lake. I let him hold my nose with one hand, my back with the other and push me under, hold me down. He jerked me out shouting that I was cleansed, purified, forgiven for all my sins.

I lived with them in an old farmhouse in the country where we prayed together three times a day, where chores, food, and secrets were shared.

At prayer they spoke in tongues, taken by a force I could not feel or see. But something possessed them as they stood in a circle, squeezed my hands, smiled tearfully at the ceiling and swayed. Something filled them, made them speak about the mystery of God, and filled them with tongues of flame. I held their hands and watched them throw back their heads, their eyes closed, throats flushed with some inner heat as tongues waggled, babbled, and prayed. Possession again. I knew the signs. I'd seen Oral Roberts, and to me it looked like the demon had gripped them, that some demon was spitting, flowing, and burning its way out into the room through their tongues.

I met a boy named Mark. He carried a green New Testament in his pocket, and he always smiled. His parents were sinners, he told me, and that was why he had run away. He was going to be a preacher one day, he said, save his parents, save all those damned souls. He could quote the Bible and told me he had the gift of the spirit. "I'll pray for you, Shirley," he said. He was tall, and I liked his smooth-looking skin, his muscled arms. He had a lean man's face, a full mouth, and wild shining green eyes.

He prayed with me whenever he found me alone outside, or busy doing some chore in a room. He would grab me, grip my head between his hands, and pull me hard to his chest. He told me if I believed, I would be reborn. I wanted that. I wanted to start a new life without dying, start all over just with a prayer.

One day his hands hurt, but I had learned they never hurt as much if you didn't fight, so I didn't move. I smelled the scent of his shirt and the medicinal smell of his soap. He pulled harder, so close I felt the bulge of him pressing in my belly. I closed my eyes and prayed that he was only praying, that the bulge between us would melt away.

"Your body is a temple," he said. "Even

125

Jesus knows that." He pushed me down and pulled my clothes off. He grinned, not seeing me, but something else beyond me, something he would have. I was a doll again, and he was ripping my head off, my legs and arms, pulling at the punched hole between my legs to get inside. He yanked off my panties and spread me on the ground in the leaves. He shoved inside me crying, pushing me harder, until I was a dead thing squashed deep into the ground again. "Sweet Jesus," he said, crying "Oh yes, oh yes." Then finally the shudder and moan that I knew meant it was over. He was up without a word. He yanked his pants closed, turned, and was gone.

By chance one day I saw Ruby at the park, sitting in a circle, passing a joint around with her friends under the trees. I told her I needed a place to stay, asked if I could stay with her, begged her, cried, and said she was my sister and she had to help me. She led me back to her circle, showed me to her friends, Dan and Linda who sold pot and played in a local rock band. They were married, Ruby said. They had their own apartment and would give me a place to crash for a while. "Just a little while, man," they said. Ruby made a deal, gave them cash and a bag of pot, and then I was passed off from hand to hand. "A couple weeks is all we can handle, man," he said. I prayed that in a couple of weeks my mother would be out of the hospital and I could go home. "Deal," Ruby said, closing up her beaded leather purse. "Shirley's no hassle, man. She's quiet. She won't eat much. You'll hardly know she's there."

I slept on their couch at night and hid my blanket and pillow in the closet for the day. I lived in the cracks, hardly ate, and tried to stay out of the light, like a mouse, a bug, some unavoidable and annoying thing that lived in the woodwork, that wouldn't do much harm. I stayed outside when they were home, scavenged my meals of peanut butter crackers, soup, and cereal when they left or went to bed. I tried to make myself a simple thing to forget.

One evening I came back to find them gone, the door shut and locked. I knocked and waited, got hungry, bored, and sleepy, then gave up and went upstairs to where I knew two women lived. They were always home. I stood at their door and listened to the TV blaring, heard them talking inside. I'd seen them around the apartment building. They always wore tight clothes and red lipstick, even when they took out the trash.

I knocked, and the older one opened it, her

hair gleaming that dyed black color, and one hand holding a cigarette as she leaned out the open door. "What's up, honey," she said.

"I'm locked out." I bit my lip to keep from crying.

She shook her head, disgusted it seemed, but she sighed and said, "Come on in. I'm Lois, and that's Dimples over there on the phone."

I'd seen Dimples sunbathing out back before with her cut-off jeans rolled high and her big loose breasts spreading like warm white dough under and out of the tight border of her halter top. Dimples. She did have a nice smile sometimes.

I looked at her bare foot propped up and stretching against the wall, saw the red toenails that matched her lips and chipped fingernails. Dimples was frowning. She wouldn't look up at me as she listened to a voice from the brown phone tucked under her chin while she rubbed Vaseline into her heel and ankle, then stroking the traces of the grease up her leg.

"Have a seat," Lois said. I sat and watched *The Mod Squad* gang run down a dark alley on TV. "I know you," Lois called from the kitchen. "You stay with those hippies downstairs." I heard her open a bottle and come back in. I looked up and took the Coke she offered, and watched her drink deeply from a bottle of beer. "Honey, you look beat."

"I am," I said.

She walked across the room, shook her head, stared out the window into the dark, and said, "Those two are lucky to find their own way home, much less think about you." She left the room again, and I watched Dimples shift her weight, prop the other foot up and slap a glob of Vaseline onto her other pink and wrinkled heel.

Lois came back offering me a blue pill in her palm. She looked at me, saying "Don't worry. It's prescription. It's mild and will help you relax and go to sleep."

She watched me hold it and study it as if by looking I would know if it was safe. "But I want to go home," I said, wanting my real home, my mother, my life.

She handed me the Coke. "Take this for now and get some rest. I'll wake up when I hear them come back in."

I swallowed it and let her lead me to the bedroom. I sat on top on the bedspread, took off my shoes, lay down and let her cover me with another quilt. "You'll be asleep in no time." But I was already feeling the pull of sleep like gravity as I watched the light from the next room shrink to the bright narrow crack of the closed door.

I woke to a man sitting heavily on the edge of the bed, his hand stroking up and down my back, smoothing my hair. I sat up. He was stocky and built like a bulldog with thick muscles at his neck and arms. "What do you want!" I yelled, but I knew. I had seen him working on his car in the driveway. I'd seen him turn his head, raise his eyes to follow me.

"Shh," he said, stroking my wrist and squeezing my hand. I heard Lois talking in the next room, heard the noise of a Gravy Train commercial. "I'm Jesse. You're in my bed, little girl." He held the back of my head with his hand, moved closer, and nuzzled my face. "Just like Goldilocks," he said. "But don't worry, I'm a nice old bear."

"No." I tried to back across the bed, but he grabbed at my leg. I held a pillow to my body, hoping to hide my crotch, my neck, and nipples, knowing that would be the next place he would reach. "No," I said. "Don't touch me. Leave me alone."

Lois called in like a tired mother, "Jesse, you

get in here and leave that girl alone." He looked at me, reaching for my shoulder.

"Jesse!" Lois stood in the doorway. "Jesse, she's a kid. Leave her alone if she don't want to mess with you."

He stood. "The little cunt is in my bed."

I stood and pulled on my shoes, squinting in the hard overhead light Lois had suddenly flipped on. I ran, hearing him yell, "What's she doing in my bed if she don't want it." I got out and stood shaking in the hallway, waiting in the silence of my locked apartment door. I could hear them still arguing upstairs as I sat and waited with my eyes closed. Then I heard light footsteps. I looked up saw the bare feet of Lois coming at me, frowning and shaking her head. She stepped over me, unlocked the door, and shoved it open. "Get on in. Jesse's the resident manager, honey. You be careful. Remember, he's always got the key."

I went in and locked the door behind me. I slept on the floor of the closet, made a bed of coats, pillows, and blankets, and slept like a mouse, heart fluttering, listening, ready to bolt at any noise. I thought how easy it was to say no. The word had leapt out my mouth like a frog. "No." That was all I had to do. But I knew it wasn't really that simple, knew it wouldn't be so easy without Lois there like a mother, a real mother saying, "Jesse, you leave that girl alone."

"No, no, no." I'd say it forever now. I curled up tightly in the coats and blankets, listened to the floor creak above me, the TV droning, water running, the toilet flush. I could hear his heavy feet thudding like a giant. "No, no, no," I said, not knowing then it was only the beginning, that I would spend years clenched tight, defying entry. I'd spend years fighting, saying no even to my boyfriend, the one I wanted, the one I couldn't let have me even when he got in. I was in the eye of a storm screaming no, knocking down any chance for love in my flight, trapped in the center of my own dark storm.

*   *   *

My mother came back from the hospital, skinny and pale, one kidney gone. The parties returned with the bottles of whiskey, cherry vodka, and gin, the paper bags of Bactine for sniffing, the dancing and candles, the circles of smoke. But I was safe this time locked behind the door sealed shut with a knife.

I thought I was safe, but anyone can break a window. Anyone with the power and the authority could break it all wide open; I knew that soon they would come. Daily I watched the window for the slow-cruising unmarked cars, the detectives, the sure-to-come-sometime police. Nightly, I dreamed of crashing glass, and I mentally practiced how I would run. Twice they'd tried raiding the house looking for drugs, runaways, stolen merchandise, any kind of proof that my mother was running a disorderly house. "Disorderly house?" she'd say laughing, as if they thought she were guilty of not pairing up socks, or drying the dishes, not vacuuming up the dustballs that collected under the couch.

In my dream I would hear them in the distance, the boots and radio static with barking voices like Nazi soldiers tearing through a house to find the doomed Jews. But I wouldn't get caught like Anne Frank. I would get away, grow up, and one day I'd tell the world what I knew. Every night as I struggled to sleep, I'd run through the plan in my mind. When I heard them crash through the front door, I'd slide open the window. I had prepared for this, greasing it with Crisco to make sure it would move without screeching and that it wouldn't stick. I would be up and out, across the yard and into the woods in five seconds, if I didn't pause to worry, if I didn't get caught. I would take my secret path through the trees, take the long way around my neighbor's fence, then crouching, hurry up the side of the yard, and slip in their concrete storage closet to wait there, hidden like a rat.

I was sleeping safely with my brother Glenn when the glass crashed. He was ten, had dropped acid, sniffed Bactine, and smoked pot, but he had never had a bed of his own. He slept with me, quiet, peaceful, and safe. He liked to watch me lock the door with my butcher knife. I told him we were pirates, that our bed was our ship, that strangers would fear us and never try to hurt us as we sailed safely in our bed alone. But this night a man yelled and crashed the glass with his stick, scattering shards over our blankets. I woke, head pounding to the sound of my brother's scream.

He sat straight up in the dark, rolled off his side of the bed, pulled the knife free, and threw it as he ran toward his mother in the living room where she slept with her man, where I heard the cops already shouting, kicking in the door.

I lifted the top blanket to slide the broken glass away and folded the cloth over. Leaning,

I looked out the window, seeing nothing but darkness, the bush beneath me, the woods beyond. I started to jump, but remembered my shoes. I crawled across the bed, reached to the floor for my sandals, pulled them on, jumped through the broken window and ran.

In seconds I was in the woods, crouching, glancing behind me for a cop, a police dog, the flash of a gun. I listened for screams and sirens, but heard nothing but the sound of crickets, the wind in the trees. I sucked in gulps of air as if I were drowning. It stuck in my throat where a knot was pounding, the blood roaring in my head as I ran.

I ran quickly past my turtle graveyard, and past the mossy rock where I had once sat and hid. Out of the woods and into my neighbor's yard, I crawled across the grass low as a snake. I ran for the storage shed, slid in the door, gripped the cool wall, letting it hold, then envelope me. They would never find me. I was nothing but a cold dead concrete wall.

I watched the house, tried to imagine what they'd found: the pot in the trash can, the pills wrapped in plastic in the toilet tank, the stash in the box of Hungry Jack Pancake Mix. It took time to search a house. I tried to count the police cars in the driveway, watched the pulsing red and blue lights, listened to the radio static breaking up the air of my yard. I saw them lead her outside, and toward the white unmarked car with gleaming headlights. I couldn't tell who else they were taking, couldn't see if they were arresting all of them, even taking Sally and Glenn away for living in a disorderly house. I listened to the sound of police radio voices, engines revving, and the quiet dead grating sound of gravel under tires as they pulled out, the headlights piercing the dark narrow road as they drove away.

Slipping through the crack in the door, I moved toward the hedge and squeezed through the gate. I went to the side of the house, hid in the bushes, and listened for a sound inside. I heard Ruby's voice saying, "It's all right. Don't worry, Glenn. They've gone away."

I heard a car and saw it crawl around the wooded curve, one last unmarked car, slowly passing, and followed by the shape and low rumbling sound of my daddy's truck. I sat in the dirt, and cried as I saw the red taillights flicker like demon eyes as he braked beyond the house, rolling down the steep dark hill.

I went in and saw the shattered room. I saw

Ruby rubbing Glenn's shoulders as he sat on the dining room table, leaning against her, letting her stroke the back of his head. They looked up, and we stared at each other without saying a word, surrounded by torn cushions, tipped chairs, broken dishes, and curtains pulled from rods. I moved through to the kitchen, felt them watch me as if I were a ghost, returning to see where the battle was fought and how the enemy had won.

"What happened?" I said.

Ruby shook her head as Glenn sat on the dining room table, propped up, stiff and blank as a toy. "They took her," Ruby said.

I watched Glenn chew his lip. "And they took Ronnie and Sally too."

"Sally?" I asked wondering why they would take a thirteen-year-old girl. I yelled at Ruby, "Why didn't they take you?" wishing she would sink suddenly in a hole and disappear. She was the one who had taught Momma how to sell drugs. "Why didn't they take you?" I said again. I wanted to beat her, smash her into a wall and pound her face.

"They sold to a narc," Ruby answered. "The pigs didn't find anything. They just came in, tore things up, and took them to jail."

"Who's the narc?" I said, my memory scanning all the faces that had passed through my house. It would have to be someone we thought was a friend if Sally had sold him drugs. "Bastard." I kicked my foot against a chair, picked it up, and threw it across the room. Glenn let out a cry and started sobbing. I jumped to hold him, pushed Ruby aside, and hugged him, whispering, "I'm sorry, baby. Don't worry. It's okay."

Ruby took a joint from her pocket, lit it up, shrugged at me, and walked away. I watched her face squinch as she inhaled, held her breath, and shook the match out with a quick jerk of her hand.

I pulled Glenn toward me. "Come on back to bed and try to get some sleep." But he sat, stiffly, as if glued to the table. "Come on," I said. "You hungry?" He looked up. "Come to the kitchen, and I'll make hot chocolate and a peanut butter-jelly sandwich. Would you like that?" We watched Ruby walk out the front door to smoke her joint on the stoop.

I took him under the arms, scooted him off the table, and helped him figure out where to step across the scattered mess on the floor.

In the kitchen I picked up a saucepan, rinsed it in the sink, filled it halfway with cold milk, and put it on the stove. Glenn stood with his arms crossed over his chest, watching the cold milk heat as I looked for peanut butter, jelly, and the bread.

I turned to him and asked, "Do you want me to cut off the crust?" I held the slice of bread in front of him. "The crust, you want me to cut off the crust?" No answer. "Tell me. Do you want little triangles sandwiches or a fold-over?" He took the bread and folded it, bit a hole out of the middle, opened it, looked at the hole, and stared back at me.

I got the peanut butter and chocolate syrup from the cabinet. "We'll have a nice snack," I said as if I were talking to a deaf stranger and not my brother, Glenn. I put the peanut butter jar in front of him, opened it, and handed him a spoon. He had always liked to eat peanut butter from the jar. But he only gripped the spoon in his hand and watched. I swirled the chocolate syrup in the milk seeing the color change. Lowering the heat, I turned to him. "I'll make a fold-over," I said. I slapped the peanut butter and jelly on the bread with his spoon, folded it over and put it in his hand. I found two cups and poured out the steaming chocolate milk. "Careful, let it cool." He sipped his hot chocolate, and I watched his eyes lower against the steam as his face disappeared behind the cup's rim. I knew then it would be our last late night snack.

* * *

Imagine a dark hall, gray concrete walls, naked bulbs hanging on black wire, a dirt brown linoleum floor worn in the center, dust collecting in the corners along the grimy line between brown floor and gray wall. I didn't want to look up to the light above me, fearing I'd see women caged like in the movies, locked and yipping, howling like abandoned dogs. I walked, kept my eyes on the floor, went down concrete steps, turned a corner into another hallway. "Wait here," the guard said, pointing to a rough wooden bench in front of a thick green metal screen. She walked away, and I sat, looking at the green metal cage. I tried to see in it but saw nothing beyond the dark holes. "Mom?" I said. Nothing. Just the distant clanking sounds of metal doors, footsteps, buzzers, and bells.

I saw a crack of light as a door on the other side of the screen opened. A guard prodded my mother in. When the door closed, I saw only the shadowed shape of her shoulder and her long, thick, dark hair.

"Momma."

"Shirley," she said, tired mostly and also, I could hear, annoyed.

I went to the screen, put my hands across it, hoping she'd put her palm up and try to feel me through the screen the way they did in movies. But she just sat there in the dark. "Are you all right?" I leaned closer. "Momma?"

"I'm all right," she said. "It's cold here. We've got bugs too. You know how I hate bugs."

I was crying. "Momma, why did you do this?"

"Stop it," she answered. "You know damn well your daddy did this to me."

He didn't, he didn't, I wanted to scream. But I knew he did. I had seen the truck, knew he had clued the cops onto my mother to get back for her lover, her life. But I also knew my mother sold the drugs, got my sister Sally to do it, told us all to sell to help buy groceries and pay the bills. I tried to see the woman I called my mother behind that dark screen and wondered what would Shirley Temple do in a situation like this? I sucked in gulps of air until finally I could open my mouth without screaming, "Do you need anything?" I asked.

"Out," she said. "I need out of my god-damned life."

I listened to the distant sound of guards talking, the sound of buzzers, keys, my mother's breath.

"Don't talk crazy, Momma. Nobody really wants to die."

She sobbed, bent over, and cried the hard high crying sounds of a girl. "Your daddy did this," she wailed. "Your daddy did this to me."

* * *

Imagine a tiny garden, six by six feet, a tomato plant, some broccoli, Brussels sprouts, potatoes, parsley, a few stalks of corn that I harvested too soon. I ate the two-inch ears, crunching raw and sweet, standing there in the yard. My garden was fed with organic mulch from the compost heap, and protected from bugs by my homemade mix of vinegar, garlic and cayenne pepper. I was a vegetarian and pure. I did yoga, rhythmic breathing, and chanted a mantra twice a day to keep myself intact.

I told no one that my mother was in Nashville at a state penitentiary serving her seven-year time. I was sixteen, alone in a falling down house, rotting window frames propped in place with boards, ice forming inside the glass on cold nights, the ceiling sagging in the bedroom.

It was the man I called my daddy's house, but he let me live there, the way somebody lets a rabbit live in the bushes of their back yard. I lived there, carefully and quietly, knowing any minute that he could come take it away. I stayed, grateful day to day for a house, my doll's house, my underground house above land. I put plastic over the broken window and stuffed rags in the cracks around the frames. I worked after school at the Woolworth's soda fountain, making sundaes, serving sand- wiches and hard frozen, greasy, crinkle-cut french fries.

I still slept with a butcher knife locking my door. I had a life, my life, was no doll now to be picked up, played with, and put back on a shelf. I washed my clothes in the bathtub, hung them on the line outside on warm days or strung them over the heater in my room when it was cold. My house, my laundry, my bed, my kitchen, my life.

My daddy sometimes came to the soda foun- tain where I worked. He never sat at the counter with Sally and Glenn who always plopped down immediately and fumbled with the sugar packets, arranging them in squares and rows only to scoop them up again and shove them in the little wire holder when he gave them the signal that it was time to go. He stood behind them, gave the order for two chocolate milkshakes to go. I always made them myself, extra thick, with a little added whipped cream and a cherry on top. Glenn and Sally liked that. They always took their shakes with both hands, looked at me and smiled. He had the money ready. Then leaving he always left me a ten-dollar tip. I wouldn't meet his eyes as I shoved the bill in my pocket. I could see too well the man who had chased my brother around the house, my brother screaming, "No I don't want to go with you! I want my momma! I want to stay home." Daddy had chased Glenn like a dog that had broken loose from its chain. He ran after him yelling, "She's in jail, goddamn it. Now stop this shit and get in that truck!"

I had packed Glenn's things in a brown grocery bag like Daddy told me to do. I folded and stacked his jeans, t-shirts, underwear, toothbrush, his stuffed monkey named Wamby. I sat on the porch with the bag filled to the brim, Wamby's soft furred head resting against my knee and watched Glenn run in circles until Daddy yanked him up, held him like a sack of potatoes at his side, then shoved him in the truck and slammed the door. "Give me his stuff, Shirley," he called. I ran to him with the paper bag bouncing against my chest, and I held it close, hugged it and tried to breathe the smell of it before I lifted it to his hands. He shoved the bag between them in the truck. He ignored Glenn who was sobbing into his fists. He didn't look at me as he climbed into the truck and shut the door. He frowned, jerked the ignition, revved the engine, and turned to look down the drive as he backed out and drove away. He took Glenn and didn't bother to ask were Ruby was, or if she'd stick around to take care of me. He left as if I were a grown-up, as if that falling down house were mine to pay for when something broke.

So I wouldn't meet his eyes. I looked only at the money and the thick calloused hand that pushed it across the counter until I picked it up. I said nothing until I heard Sally say, "Bye, Shirley."

I watched them walk away until they disappeared behind the shelves of the store, thinking: Yes, go on. That's what I want. Leave me alone.

145

IV

When my mother went to prison she said she had her first out-of-body experience. The guards led her across the prison yard on a narrow sidewalk, and she saw her building ahead, a low flat red brick place. She felt the two matrons beside her, could hear the whoosh of cloth rubbing on the fat one's thighs. Then she said she simply stepped back and up a little, floating somehow, walking between them the same as ever and yet floating above. She looked down, saw the dandruff sticking to the thick oily brown hairs on one head, and on the other saw the stretched stiff fabric of her navy hat. She said she felt fine then, peaceful, big as the world. She said it happened all the time while she was locked up in Nashville, and she wasn't even doing drugs, not a drink, nothing but aspirin for her backache sometimes. She called it liberation as if it were a spiritual thing. But I knew desperation when she told it. I knew that numb panic, the pain that becomes so thick and heavy it spills over your senses and pushes you out of your own skin. I never told her what I thought, never said, you were unhappy, Momma. You were going out of your head.

I knew because I'd been there. I'd lived as a ghost watching the world move by, no more substantial than a curling column of warm steam or a thick damp breeze. I've been a ghost in the foreign world of the living ones who seem to have had a map of life in their heads. Sometimes I'd feel the presence of the world, like something vaguely remembered, recognizing a few living moments, like going home on a metro and recalling that back at the waiting platform I had seen a familiar face in the crowd.

I know why the ghosts wail. They have been robbed and lack the body that could grab hold and take something back. They hold nothing, are reduced to thin cries and moans most will mistake for rain, or wind, some familiar, natural sound. A ghost is robbed, senses stripped, soul abandoned, cut off from its body like a decapitated chicken, the body flapping its wings. It runs in circles, blood gushing from the wound, while the head lies in the grass, separate, watching it all from a distance, eyes blinking, dead, but without knowing its life is already gone.

I knew that my mother in prison was a dead ghost, not floating free. In pain, she stepped out of herself and told herself she was above and beyond the ground, the brick, the fence, the wall. But I knew that if she had to go back and feel it all again, she would refuse to take on that body of pain.

I know that free-floating numb bubble of a self that hovers safe and distant. I know the distance from pain when you are already dead. I have felt the slow swelling rise away from myself, suddenly so big and light and peaceful watching the wretch down there struggling to sleep and rest. The big self hovers like Glenda, the good witch in her soft bubble of light, kisses the poor child's forehead for luck, says to take comfort in charms: the kiss of a witch and the dead woman's stolen shoes. And the little self, trapped, glued to the ground by gravity, says, "Yes, I'll go on," because that is all she can do. Chin up, eyes, forward, feet moving on.

I could never help but slip my bare feet into my mother's shoes. Clomp, clomp, my toes pinched down for leverage against all that extra sliding space, knees wobbling in her heels. I would sneak in her closet, breathe the scent of wool and perfume on her dresses, the leather smell of belts and purses. I liked the slight sweat stink, the faint human odor rubbed deep in the lining of her soles. I liked the aquamarine heels best; they glimmered and glowed, felt sleek and slick as oil in my hands. I pulled them out, slipped them on, and stood to admire my longer legs. I stuck my fingers in the gap in the back to measure the distance between me and my mother, and I'd stretch my feet to try to make them grow.

*   *   *

At sixteen I lived alone with only mice, roaches, and one wild cat. I never knew its name, but called it Momma Cat because her belly was huge and tight swinging wide and low to the ground when she walked. I had seen her mating one night in the yard under the porch light, screaming and yowling in what I thought must be pain. He crouched over her, gripping her shoulders with his claws tearing at the back of her neck, and she writhed against him, muscles clenching, screaming out. They clutched, clung, and wrestled, like those lizards I had seen before, procreating, copulating, making love. They yowled until finally he'd had enough and jerked out, tearing her inside as she fought against a penis designed to penetrate, ejaculate, and tear out only at his will. He leapt from her without looking back. She skulked, walked low, tail swishing, eyes bright. She growled and kept glancing back toward the darkness where he had run. Then slowly her legs stretched as she stood a little taller with each step, feeling the freedom of her muscles moving with her own will. She straightened up, glared, then suddenly, she ran.

Momma Cat was a wild thing that lived on what she could catch, scavenge, and steal. She grew fatter, surviving somehow on the cans of cat food I brought when I had the extra change. She managed. Cats do. As I did, as anybody, she did the best she could.

Then she ate her babies. I never saw it happen, just the bone and fur remained scattered on the floor each day I came in from school. I stood in the kitchen and put my school books on the counter, then saw it in the corner: a tiny furred head, eyes gouged out, skin peeled back on white bone, veins dangling like colored wires where a neck could have been.

Momma Cat skulked out of her closet, haunches bone thin, big round wild yellow eyes, ears back. She circled the skull then swatted it across the floor, looked up at me, then walked out the open door.

Only possession could make a mother eat her babies. I thought a doctor might give me another reason. But I never asked anyone. Possession. I knew the signs. My cat ate all her babies, and I just swept the parts up daily into the dustpan, and carried them to the woods. I never said a word to anyone. I was too ashamed.

*   *   *

When my mother died the doctor said her bones were so thin they didn't show up on the x-rays. I wondered what had held her up? The woman had no bones. What held her? Habit? Denial? Will?

Her bones had leeched away with the loss of calcium. Her womb, kidneys, bladder, stomach, intestines had all slowly filled with cancer, rotted away, and left her, a dry-skinned casing of blood, fluid, a heart that kept pounding,

151

and a brain that kept making plans. She held the world in her clawed grip, insisting: "God-damn it, I'm still alive!"

She had told me once when I was a girl that she'd die young, that her family was doomed. Then she promised, "But don't worry, Shirley, even after I'm dead I'll be around you. Your momma will be right there every second of the day."

"No," I said, "I don't want you hanging around me dead." Then she pushed me from her lap, shoved me from the rocker as if I were an insect that had looked harmless but suddenly stung. She reached for her drink and a magazine. "Go outside and play," she said without looking up to see my face.

They called my mother the one who wouldn't die. They were amazed that she kept floating up from comas, settling down again, and speaking clearly after seizures so strong she shook the wires and tubes loose from the bed. But she died finally, far beyond the family curse that she would die before the age of thirty-five. She lived on almost twenty years more, lived somehow, demanding to be washed and cared for like those dolls she once kept burying and digging up. Her secret of success: "I just live to love my babies," she'd say with a sweet wise smile as if that were all she'd ever done, as if this were some kind of deep and ultimate truth.

Really? I wondered, never daring to ask: When did you start living to love? I didn't want to make her cry and try to defend herself. I would do anything not to see my parents cry. "I'll be good, I'll be good," I had always whispered to myself the way any normal child simply draws a breath. "I'll do my best to please."

I watched my mother, fetal, curled in a coma, eyes protruding, hands drawn like bird claws, lips pursed thin, tight and pale. I saw de-evolution in that hospital bed, saw a primate fetus take shape in my mother, a bird, reptile, fish. Her body parts were going piece by piece, the second kidney taken, along with the cancer-eaten remains of ovaries, uterus, cervix, the womb where she carried me once, my pink warm fertile blood-and-water home. Gone the bladder tissue, muscle, blood. Then finally, her bones went, not one by one but in a slow fade. Calcium leeched into dialysis, a gland failed that could stop the flow. The suck and pull of the machine was wasting her away as it cleansed the toxins from her blood.

153

Her brain kept firing, liver filtered, heart pumped, lungs pulled oxygen from the air. Modern maintenance techniques kept her taped together. A blue plastic bag sealed to her skin around the intestine that protruded pink and alive, like a wide-mouthed worm. Another bag hung, sealed, a flap there like a blue fin, her disposable bladder. Her bags could be emptied, cleaned and rinsed until the seals wore out and they started leaking. Then they were wrapped in tissue, pushed deep in the trash can, and thrown quickly away.

My mother had a fascination for the engineering and mechanics of her medical maintenance things. Three times a week she drove herself to the clinic until she was so weak that we had to take turns driving her, helping her into the easy chair in front of the TV in that fluorescent-lit, falsely cheerful, whirring dialysis room. She said, "Staying alive is the job I do." She called it going to work, said it could be worse: at least she was alive. "I want to live to love my babies," she said.

Why now? I wondered, remembering the mother who'd cut her wrists, taken overdoses of pills, who put a gun to her head and threatened to kill herself and us more times than I could count. Why struggle for life now? You were healthy then, your body was fine, not in constant pain.

I couldn't see the inner wiring of her brain, her thoughts and heart any more than I could see the spark and flaming danger of those wires my daddy twisted together and hid in the attic. She had a plan as he did. She was rigged somehow for a profit of destruction. She thought she could get something in dying, just the way they thought they could gain when they burned their own house down.

Watching her I wanted to rip my own head off to stop knowing her pain. I wondered what I'd find inside. I knew how to do it, how to push the back of the head, hitch fingertips firmly under the bone base of the skull, then pull, snap, pop, roll the head free. It would all be over then. Maybe like a doll I would feel nothing at all.

Mothers kill their children. It happens all the time. A mother cuts a daughter's throat to spare her certain pain. It happens: pans of boiling water fly; a locked house burns in the night; the barrel of a gun presses gently into some boy's temple, then explodes. A woman trapped, desperate, and beaten, doing the best she can with that wild ripping urge to have an effect on someone's, anyone's life. It's easy to kill a child, just takes a second to slip a knife, squeeze a trigger, hold a head under water, silence it pushing down.

Break a bone and you don't hear only the dry dull snap, but a scream. Hold the bone to your ear and hear the blood black tidal wave roar up, an ocean of screaming loss, grief, shrieking simple pain. Bones hold the stories of our lives like the faint circles in the sawed trunks of trees. Put your ear to the wood. Listen to the distant gnawing sound of feeding insects, the sap ebbing and trapped in the dead wood, trying without a chance to course its way back to the roots still reaching and sucking life from the deep damp earth.

They say a lobster screams when you plunge it tail first into boiling water. They say you can hear the thin high shriek, its hard jaws opening, its tiny black bead eyes rolling in its head. They tell us to do the humane thing; plunge it in head first to kill it in an instant. But I know, I've heard the silent scream under water. I know we do the humane thing simply not to hear the sound.

*   *   *

My mother knew when she was going. She lay flat on her back in her hospital bed, looked at the ceiling and seemed to see the words. "I'm leaving you this time, babies," she said, and I knew there was no holding on, no pulling her up and out this time from that black space. The fever carried her and dragged her out as we watched like sentries, standing at the corners of her bed, and saw her disappear. At the end she seemed like a shrunken leather doll, something they could have buried once as a charm in a Native American grave. She was a tiny withered thing that last day, clutching and babbling as she clawed at the sheets, tried to pull herself up from sinking into an invisible pit at the center of her bed.

"Agitation" the doctor called it, the usual wild clinging to life before sinking into death. I watched her claw at the sheets, and saw myself going under, hands clutching at the water as my possessed mother held me down. I saw her above me pushing, then suddenly below me, small and sinking into the white sheets of her bed. Her head flailed as she babbled, only now and then a meaningful phrase. "I wish ya'll would do my nails, I'm tired of looking like an old hag," she said, stretching her fingers out, straining to see the chipped polish on her nails.

Finally she stopped and let herself sink into that secret space in the room, fall through that tear in the fabric I had thought was life. I watched the heart monitor's digital numbers slow, stop, start, slow. Her death was no sudden thing, but rather a gradual ebbing, like water poured into dirt, a pool of water that sinks and disappears without really going away.

* * *

I didn't want to be the one to divide my mother's ashes into those little dime store imitation Oriental urns. It was Sally's idea to save her. Momma had said she wanted to be thrown into the lake, but Sally couldn't do it. Sally had to hold on. All of them wanted to save back a scoop of her to keep except for my daddy and me. "Let her go," I said. She was the one who said she wanted to be burned and thrown into the lake.

Sally planned a birthday dinner in honor of Momma's ashes; she decided that Mom's birthday would be the best day to save what we wanted, then throw the rest away. But I was the one who sifted through those ashes, divided her up into little urns with a spoon. I didn't want to do it, but like so many other things in my life, I did it.

I had to. Sally saw to that. It was time to leave for the lake to meet the others for the ceremony, to stand together and take turns grabbing handfuls of my mother and toss her away. Sally planned it. She went to take a shower and left me alone in the kitchen with a new row of brightly painted tiny vases and cork stoppers. I held the little urns in my hand, ran my finger over the intricate vines, the green leaves, and red blossoms. There were twelve of them with twelve tiny corks. My mother would be like a genie broken up into little bottles and sealed until someone opened them and made a wish.

"Okay, I'll do it," I said as if dividing ashes were an unwanted chore as simple as carrying out the trash. I took a breath, walked to the living room and grabbed the big smooth ceramic urn provided by the funeral home. Holding it in both hands, I carried it to the kitchen table. I saw Daddy lean back in his chair and pale. He looked at Sally's husband, both of them repulsed by me carrying my dead mother's ashes across the living room in front of the football game they insisted on watching on TV.

Sally was in the shower, her kids playing Nintendo in the back room. I smelled the ham cooking and looked over at the buffet spread with covered dishes of green beans, sweet potatoes, coconut cake, all Momma's favorite foods. We would celebrate her birthday, the first birthday after the day she died. We would light candles and have a party after we threw her ashes into the lake.

I sat at the kitchen table, placed the urn in front of me and spread my hands over the smooth lid. I felt them staring at me, their mouths twisted with disgust as they fumbled for cigarettes. I saw my daddy slam my mother's head again and again into a wall. I saw him beat her unconscious with the broken leg of a chair. Now I hoped he was afraid.

I opened the urn and reached for a spoonful of the ashes. I looked at him, smoking his cigarette as he watched me lift the lid of the urn as if I were opening a jar of pickles. "Don't worry," I said, "Momma can't hurt you now." I wished for a moment that life could be like those movies where demons let loose could slam a man against a wall.

But, of course, nothing happened, and they went back to watching an instant replay on the TV screen. I stared into the urn and saw nothing but ashes, crumbled dusty bits of white, so light, yet so heavy and dense.

I opened the urn as if it were a tomb, a vault no mortal had opened for thousands of years, and there was nothing. No sudden vengeful blast of rage. This was the truth. All that existed of her was in my mind. I sat and scooped out a bit of her, felt the dense light weight of grit in the palm of my hand. Then suddenly, as if I'd rung a dinner bell, the kids came running. "We're hungry," they called as they saw me, then paused as they tried to figure what I was doing with something that looked like a cookie jar.

"This isn't cookies," I said. They found the Oreos and Chips Ahoy in the cabinet and stood eating, crumbs flying across the floor as they watched me spill ashes on the table.

"Y'all get away from there," Daddy said. But they weren't budging. They stood, watched me roll a piece of wax paper into a funnel, then smoothly slide the ashes a bit at a time into a tiny vase.

A large chunk of something clogged the opening; I took it, put it aside. The kids moved closer, cookie crumbs falling on the table. They were so close, I could hear the chewing, could hear them breathe. "What's tha-ut?" one hollered. They pointed, moved in for a better look.

"Grandmother," I said, as if they could

understand the process of a woman reduced to ashes. They looked curious as I explained the business of sickness, death, ashes, and the story of life beyond death. "Well it's not really grandmother," I said. "It's just her body. Grandmother's soul lives forever, you know." They nodded, but they were more interested in the clumps of things, the bits of clips, and screws and staples that worked to hold my mother's body together when she was alive.

They ate more cookies, crumbs mingling with the scattered ashes. I tried to keep moving, wanted to get it over, but I couldn't help grinning at their pink fingers reaching, their complete acceptance of a dead woman's ashes on the table while they ate cookies and watched. One grabbed a tiny screw, and said, "Well, what's tha-ut?", his arm knocking over an urn.

"Careful. That was a screw they put inside Grandmother for an operation once."

"A screw?" they chimed together, their faces almost laughing, surprised, maybe a little shocked at the things grownups could do. More pieces scattered, more tiny nuts, bolts, staples, rolling up though the gravel and grit. They stood until they'd had their fill of cookies, and I told them to go on back in the bedroom

162

and play. I watched them race from the room and on to the next video game. I could hear my mother laughing just behind me, that old wild laugh she had when she danced with us in the kitchen, when she forgot her life and played. I knew she would like to see her grand-children fingering her ashes, making no distinction between ashes and crumbs.

The men sat pale and nervous, ready to bolt, it seemed, at the sign of something supernatu-ral. Only guilt could make them fear such a curse.

I carried the urn on my lap in the back seat of Sally's station wagon as we drove up to Chickamauga Lake where motor boats pulled water skiers gripping wooden handles with rope that held them firmly to the boats. The engine pulled them wildly round and round over the frothing surface of the water as if there were nothing in the world but speed and wind and water, as if it all could be forever alive.

We found the place on the north shore of the lake where she had liked to fish. There we stood in the winter mud by the lake, and I dipped my hand in the urn, grabbed a fistful of ashes, and tossed them on the blue-gray water. We heard the shlooshing sound of the tiny stones hit water and sink. Filmy thin sprays of dust hung on the surface, then washed out in the waves and finally disappeared into the glare of sunlight on dark water. We each dug our hands in the urn and tossed her out, again and again until nothing was left but what I had saved back home in those tiny vessels, neatly arranged on the counter and corked. We stood there squinting in the light, listening to the sucking sound of water as the current pulled her out.

*   *   *

My daddy is in jail now. They know him. He's been there more times than anyone cares to count. He says he likes jail. The Silverdale Workhouse. "Sil-verdale" he calls it smoothly, as if it's a resort. "Yep, I'm going back out to Sil-verdale," he says, as he sits back, almost proud. "Gonna rest up and save my money for a while." He says he likes the card games, the sitting around with the boys and "shooting the bull." He says he likes not having to do nothing but eat and sleep and go to your room.

But the warden there knows my daddy can cook, so they always give him kitchen duty. I can see him in his white cap and long white

apron, throwing pot holders, ladling out
beans, fried potatoes, cutting huge flat sheets
of cornbread—his own recipe, cornbread doc-
tored up with chopped pepper, onion, kernels
of canned corn. They like it when he comes
back to the workhouse. The eating is always
better because he cheats on the recipes, slips
good things in like spices and extra oil.

But now he is in private lockup. Sally told
me he got too generous and started giving
double dessert to the inmates. "What the hell,"
he must have said. "If a man wants two pieces
of peach cobbler, why the hell not?" He knew
that leftovers just got thrown out or carried
home with the guards. So what the hell. He
gave second rounds of desserts to his buddies,
until someone who wanted points with the
warden—someone who didn't like sweets
maybe—told on him. So he's in private lockup.
No cards, no "shootin' the bull with the boys,
no TV." This is how he pays.

He laughs about doing time in Silverdale,
swears he doesn't mind it, says that in Silverdale, if you play your cards right, you can get
whatever you want. He's not just talking either.
He's talking poker, Black Jack, five-card stud.
He winks when he tells me, "You can get anything you want." And I know this means whis-

key, drugs, dirty magazines, blow jobs, women, anything you want. "Play your cards right," he always says, "and you can get anything." Then he sits back and shrugs. He shakes his head, bites his lip and says, "And if you lose, what the hell." He laughs in that snickering way of his. "I don't give a damn. If you lose, what the hell."

I wonder if he says that in lockup, the dim little concrete room. Does he sit there laughing? Or does he close his eyes and cry? Does it matter? He is in that dark room, muttering, "What the hell. Yeah. What the hell."

V

I took the bus to college one day. I had to think about it a long time to get up the nerve. But I couldn't make BLT's and milk-shakes forever. And when I was a kid my teachers always said I was smart.

So I did it. Hazel, my boss, pushed me. She's old and has copper-red hair that she dyes, but she's still got good legs for a woman her age. She kept saying, "Shirley, you're too smart to waste your life here."

I am smart, I guess. I didn't know it until I went back to the schools and got my records. One teacher had written that I was an "exceptional child." So I took the bus and asked the driver to tell me where to get off. He was a nice man. He had those gentle, wide-open eyes. When he stopped, the bus hissed, and he smiled at me. He pointed out the open door and told me which sidewalk to take to the main campus. I stood on the last step and looked out half expecting the walkway to be shining like that road to Oz, smooth, winding, and gold. I got out and started walking the way he said. It was a regular sidewalk, tan and dirty looking, cracked and edged with grass.

I looked for the biggest, oldest building, thinking that would have to be the center of things; that would be the place to start. I watched my Dingo boots go down the sidewalk. I had saved for them a long time, used all Daddy's ten-dollar tips. I bought them because boots make me walk a little tougher and taller. They make me feel bigger, a little more solid and strong.

Then I saw it there in front of me, where all the sidewalks come together like the spokes of a wheel. I looked up at the old dark brick building, saw the turrets and little stained glass windows. It was college, just like in the movies, old and solid. Grand. That's what I kept thinking. It was a movie word: Grand. I saw the ivy growing, thick green ivy winding up and all over the wall. Just the way it was supposed to be.

I hurried up the steps, pushed open the glass door, and stood breathing in the smell of floor cleaner and cigarettes. I saw a Coke machine in the corner and a black metal trash can with an ashtray on top, dirty with mashed butts and a pink-chewed wad of gum.

I turned and watched two guys go down the street with back-packs. The guy in the denim jacket was eating an apple, and the other sipped something hot from a styrofoam cup, the steam curling up around his face. It soothed me just watching. This was the world. It was soothing and happy and warm. Sparrows were picking at a McDonald's bag that had fallen from a trash can across the street. I remembered the story in the paper about a cat that lived outside the dormitory. The students took care of it. They even collected money to get it fixed and all its shots. They took care of things in college. That's what Hazel told me. "You're smart," she said. "You'll be all right."

I watched the guys walk by, and then I sighed so hard I left a cloud on the window in front me. I drew a heart with the tip of my finger, and looked out through the clear space I made. I saw a man with gray hair and a dark suit pedaling down the street on a bike. A leather briefcase wobbled on the back of his bike. I wondered if he was a professor. Would I know him? Would he teach me things? Would he give me good grades? All I knew about college then was that people sat in classrooms and talked about books. I knew bells didn't ring, and we wouldn't have to crowd down the halls like cattle. We'd walk outside in college. We would eat apples and drink warm things and talk.

My daddy had told me that only the people in college could really vote: "Anybody can go in that booth and flip a lever," he said. "But it's only the votes in the college that count."

That day at the soda fountain when I told them I was going to try to go to college, he just slid another ten-dollar tip at me and said, "What the hell."

"You don't know a damned thing," I said and suddenly realized I was talking to the window. The heart I had drawn was beading up with water and already fading away. I looked around, hoping no one heard me talk to a window. But no one was there, just the humming Coke machine and the dull gleam from those polished brown floors.

I heard voices as a door opened down the hall, and I saw two women in skirts, sweaters, and high heels, with that done-up plastic kind of hair. One carried a coffee pot. They disappeared into a swinging door, one saying: "I told you. I told you he'd say that." The other one laughed. I tried to remember if I'd ever laughed like that, the free wild silly way girls have when they laugh with other girls.

In the movies college girls giggled late at night, eating popcorn, painting toenails, and waiting for the boys to call them on the phone. I knew I'd never laugh like that. Not even in college. I'd be the serious girl. Like the ones who wore glasses even though I didn't wear them. I'd read books and have discussions. I didn't want to go to college just to talk about boys.

I saw the women come out and walk down the hall, heels tap-tapping, still talking and laughing. I watched where they went, looked up on the wall and saw the black plastic sign that had an arrow pointing their way: "Admissions." I knew I might have to talk to them, or someone like them. That was the way it went in the normal world. I would have to talk to ladies like social workers in skirts and sweaters and heels. They would ask me questions, but they would never know me. They'd be like that social worker who used to come to our house and ask us if we ate, if we slept, if we went to school. We'd all answer the right way, Momma with her hair all brushed, and Daddy across the room in his chair, listening to everything we said. So we told her the right stories, and she made notes, and then drove away. I would watch her walk across the rocky driveway in her little white pumps. I wanted to chase her and scream: "You don't know. Come back and I'll tell you." No one ever understood.

I looked down the hall at the brick walls and the brown floor, and saw my mother in that cage in the dark basement of the county jail. I was shaking inside. I wanted to run.

Taking a breath, I walked down the hall to the women's room. I told myself to pee, wash my hands, take some breaths, focus on my heart beating, tell myself they couldn't hurt me now. I tried to relax, then pushed the door open and went into the small square room with dirty yellow tiles, green cinderblock walls, and beige metal stalls. I stepped inside one, set the latch, pulled down my jeans, sat and looked at the pale gooseflesh of my thighs. I didn't really need to pee, but felt I should try. I wanted to go in that admissions office emptied of everything I could. I didn't want to fidget, didn't want to stop in the middle of filling out forms and answering their questions, to say, "Excuse me, I need to go to the bathroom." College girls wouldn't say things like that, only little girls, shy girls in the back of an overheated classroom half full of boys; only girls locked in cars had to get someone's attention to ask to go pee.

I stared at the beige door in front of me and saw a wobbling oval peace sign like a mashed-up pie with crooked slices cut. On another wall red letters screamed: "NOW!" High above I saw a drawn penis. I gave up trying to pee and stood up to look. It wasn't a penis, but the big-nosed cartoon face of a man peering out, fingers gripping the edge of a wall as he watched from nowhere, hanging there, beneath the scrawled words: "Kilroy was here."

I didn't know what it meant. I stepped out of the stall and saw my face, calm and relieved, almost happy that the face in the mirror belonged to me. In college they wouldn't draw things like penises and boobs and butts on the walls. They had ideas like peace and women's lib, and "Kilroy was here."

I turned on the faucet and let the warm water soothe my hands. I looked in the mirror and saw my new face. It was then I changed my name. I saw the round face, the smooth skin, slightly freckled, still what some would call cute. The girl in the mirror wore a black t-shirt and a rose print handkerchief, twisted and tied like a necklace around her neck.

173

There were delicate red-pink rosebuds scattered across the white cloth black border. The girl looked pretty; she looked smart, thoughtful and sweet. Nothing like Shirley Temple, not in that black t-shirt and the handkerchief tied kind of sexy on her neck.

I looked down, saw that I wasn't really sexy, not with my flat chest, faded jeans, and those scuffed-up, square-toed boots. The face in the mirror floated in the reflection of fluorescent light. Who was she? They would want to know my story. How would I ever show them the girl behind that face, so lost and longing for someone to show her what to do, tell her who she really was?

"My name is Ivy," I said to the face in the mirror. And the face looked happy saying it, liked the word that opened her lips, sliding from her mouth. "I-VY." I saw the green ivy that grew on the brick wall outside. Ivy. Sometimes it made a wall, but it was alive. Ivy. Ivy Rivers. It was my mother's maiden name. No more daddies' names. I had taken Rivers from my mother the day I scooped up her ashes from the urn and threw her into the lake. I was Shirley Rivers then, but now it was a new face looking out.

Shirley was gone, but Momma was still in

me. I could see her in the blue-veined skin of my throat, my freckled arms, my smell, like her smell, the fresh bread scent when I put my face to the back of my hand. Momma was scattered white ashes at the bottom of the lake, but she was in me. Her stories played and re-played like a film loop, my mother, the girl who buried her babies to dig them up again, the girl who cried under the pecan tree, count-ing the stripes on her legs.

I looked in the mirror and told myself that I would never be Shirley again. She was a dead doll, only a mechanical thing made with a tape coiled in her back and speaker holes punched in her chest. She was a made thing that could say happily, "It's the best ever" while fingers pulled, penises pushed, and mouths covered her with the press of lips, whiskers, and teeth. Shirley was buried under the weight of those thighs and chests, those mouths and hands. Shirley was dead.

But Ivy could grow anywhere. It crawled up from black dirt. Tiny pale-fingered vines reached and dug into the dark brick and cracked mortar of a wall. Ivy could pull itself up and live, grow up and over a tree, a bush, a building, anything at all.

I looked at the girl named Ivy in the mirror

175

and made her practice a smile. People always liked you better if you smiled. Ivy's teeth were a little crooked, but I knew they were clean. I tried the smile, but it was too forced, false and scary. I made my face blank and thought of warm things, a towel fresh from a dryer, the oven when a cake is baking, hot cocoa made from scratch, biscuits forked open and spread with butter and jam. These were the good things once. And I would have them again.

I looked in the mirror. I looked nothing like Shirley Temple. Shirley Temple didn't have long straight hair and crooked teeth, and she never, never wore a man's black t-shirt. My mouth was really too thin to curve into a cute little doll's-mouth bow. I sighed and felt the ghost of Shirley Temple break loose with a chill, like the feeling of taking off sticky wet clothes.

I heard the door open, turned, and saw a black woman in a light blue uniform come in. The cleaning lady acted as if it were her own bathroom at home. She glanced at the sinks, with a quick sweep of her hand lifted the plastic liner of the trash can, then swinging it like a purse, she walked along the room and looked inside each stall.

She caught me staring in the mirror, but she

must have caught a hundred girls doing the same kind of thing. I straightened the strap of my bag on my shoulder, then looked inside to make sure my papers were there. I fingered the black and white photocopy of my birth certificate, my high school transcript, the newspaper story of my mother's drug bust and the obituary that told the public that "Momma B" was out of business. Not just locked up this time, my mother was dead. I snapped the bag shut, squeezing it at my side. It was a leather bag painted with bright butterflies and flowers, ugly I thought, but I carried it because Momma had made it for me while she was in jail.

The woman was rinsing a sink, but I felt her eyes watching me. I turned, looked straight in her face, and announced, "I'm going to college."

She turned off the faucet, tightened her lips, looked at me and said, "Yeah, well you standing in my toilet now, and I got a sign out there says this toilet is closed for cleaning." She stepped back and waited for me to leave.

"God damn bitch!" Daddy would have said. She was about my mother's age. She was somebody's mother. She had a wedding ring and that tired bored look, but she could have once been a pretty woman like my friend's momma, Georgia Hanes. I could hear the words. "No one should hit a momma." I turned away, walked toward the door, then stopped and looked back at her. "No one should hit," I said.

She was opening the paper towel holder with a little silver key. She stopped and turned to me. "No one should hit anybody," I said. "You don't even know me."

She shook her head and turned back to the paper towel holder, pulling the front open and staring at the small stack of those rough brown folded towels. "You get on with your talk, girl," she said. "I got work to do."

* * *

My roommate in the dormitory thinks that I'm a witch. She's from West Virginia, and her daddy is a preacher like Oral Roberts. She says he has the power to call demons out and calls on Jesus to heal. She stares at me in the morning when I sit on my bed, lean against the concrete block wall, close my eyes, and meditate. I can feel her. I open my eyes just a peek and see her looking at me from a corner on her bed, her knees pulled to her chest under her homemade quilt. Her grandmother made it, she said. "I don't have a grandmother," I told her. "I don't have a mother. I had three daddies once, but I never knew my real dad."

She stares at me, but I smile because I am alive now, and there's no telling what a living girl named Ivy might say.

I don't tell her I was a doll once. She wouldn't hear it anyway. She thinks I am a witch. But I told my teacher. I told her in that writing sample on the first day, and now she watches me when I'm working, and she always calls on me when I raise my hand. I think she likes me. She told me she thought Ivy was a very lovely name. Lovely. Ivy. I have a lovely name.

The teacher lets us write. Free writing, she calls it. But I've learned that free does not mean easy. To write is to dig myself up, wash the dirt from my mouth, clean and press my clothes. To write free I have to struggle to spit the stones out, wipe the dirt and tiny bugs from my mouth so I can speak.

"Tell your family history," the teacher said one day. "Your mother, father, just tell me who they are, what they are like, what they do for a living." I froze. This wasn't free. She wanted something, wanted me to give something from me.

To write, I think, is to be held down and tortured in a small room underground. To write is to be your own inquisitor lashing, burning, pulling the rack tighter, making the muscles stretch, joints separate, bones break, release.

I press my own ear to my mouth, and I hear the ripping scream, the gasping breath, the cry and sigh and whisper to be killed or freed.

"Confess, confess, confess, and it will go easier. All you have to do is say yes, it is me." The leather cuts my wrist, back spasms on the rack.

I am a caught fish. The hook tears my mouth. I flinch and writhe, try to tear myself free, but the hook is set. I've swallowed it, and it won't come up now without ripping some little piece of flesh. There is no way to win. To confess is a self-inflicted gutting, to remain silent a self-made bomb wired to my belly and set to explode. I bend close to my desk, breath held against the awful smell of my own words. Like my Sybil, a living thing once thrown down to drown in a sewer, a dead thing rotting and trapped. I could see the man I called my daddy stirring the gray sludge in the heat.

"Just tell the facts about your family," the teacher said. "Don't worry. It's only a writing sample. Watch your spelling and your grammar though."

I know I won't get out until I tell, and so I

do it. My body coils and spasms, but I throw it out, nose stinging, eyes burning, mouth twisting, choking on the hot bitter taste. I see bits of my own flesh ripped pink brown and floating like shreds of liver on a plate. They plop out and settle in pools of water and blood, and wait. I tell myself that this telling might kill me, might rip out all my organs and leave me barely able to breathe. "It might kill you," I think, "but it's the only way you'll live."

* * *

To write is to cast a line out, reel it in slowly, cast again, reel back, cast, reel, expecting nothing but being ready to yank in the first hit. Then it strikes, and you feel the shudder rise up from the muscles fighting hook and line under water. The tremor moves up the rod, spreads electric through hands, arms, shoulders and knocks hard in your chest. You keep the tip up, line taut but not too much, keep the tension strong and steady as you pull. Then you see the fish break, still fighting. You watch it beat the frothing water, dive, disappear and surface again twisting in the light as you pull and try to identify the type, size, and weight of what you didn't know existed until it hit.

Sometimes, it is a slick rainbow trout that you hook, pull in and eat. Sometimes, it is a tiny, throw-back rockfish, barely enough to fry and suck the bones, or a minnow that pulls and steals your bait. But then there is the un-named unknown one, sharp-toothed, slick, and muscled, and that is all you know. It changes, writhing, defying your grip as you hold it, but transforming every minute, making you a liar as you give it a name. But you hold on, feel the slick body, the sharp fin, muscle's flexing twist. Then suddenly you feel the rip and push against your palm as it breaks, slips free and arcs in the air, and with barely a ripple dives under to feed and breed in the dark water below.

My name is Ivy. No. Shirley. No.

Free writing, she called it. Tell your family story. That is all you have to do.

I write, "My mother. My mother is white rocks and ashes scattered at the bottom of the lake." I skip a line, then write, "I never knew my daddy, but I had three."

My family story? What? What is one thing I know? I look at my notebook paper. I write Ivy/Shirley in the top right-hand corner of the page. I want to write beneath the name, "ex-

182

ceptional child." But I don't. This is a family story. Not just me.

I write that my mother was a woman sometimes and sometimes she was possessed. I write that now she is partly corked and saved in little vases and partly scattered at the bottom of a lake. I write I never knew my daddy but I had three. I write that I don't have aunts or uncles, that I have no grandparents. They are all dead. It is a family curse, I say.

I hear the humming white light above me. I see the flickering one in the corner that makes me feel dizzy, makes me want to close my eyes and sleep.

My mother told me stories. She rocked me, stroked my arm softly when she was not possessed. I look at the clock and see I have ten minutes left, and that I have only written a few lines when I was supposed to fill at least a page. Others are already handing their family stories in, smiling, and walking away.

I stare at my paper. I hear my pulse, my heart, my rushing blood.

I close my eyes and see my mother's panties. She tells me the story, as she strokes my arm. I see her panties; soft, white and folded in the dark space of his pocket. I see his hand reach in, softly rub and squeeze. I press my black

183

ink pen on the faint blue line, see the whiteness stretch out like a straight open road. I grip the pen and tell myself it's easy. I can say it, but I'm not supposed to. I can say it now because my mother is dead.

I know it isn't what the teacher wants. But I'm in college, and she said she would be the only one to read it. "Free writing," she said. "Just tell the truth. It isn't for a grade." I watch her already reading someone's paper. She looks a little sleepy. She looks awfully bored.

I look back to my new blank page. Okay. My name is Ivy, and I'm a girl, a live one now. My mother is white rocks and scattered ashes at the bottom of the lake. I did it. I scooped her in tiny urns for the others and threw my share away. Now I cannot be my mother's living doll. I have my own mouth, and I no longer eat the dirt. I open my mouth now and things fly out. And only what I want goes in.

I am alive, and I can tell the story. I see her panties slip into his pocket, feel the soft darkness there. "Just keep the pen moving," the teacher said. "The rest of it will flow." I press the pen to paper, see the straight white road stretching out to the red-lined margin, and I write:

"When my grandfather died . . ."